COMPLETELY YOURS

Fictionalized Love Stories of Real-Life Couples

by

CRYSTAL JOY

Edited by: Daisycakes Creative Services

Cover design by: Goonwrite.com

Interior Design and Formatting by: BB eBooks

Copyright 2016 Crystal Joy

Print Edition

ISBN-13: 978-1548894993

ISBN-10: 1548894990

For my husband. Without you, the love of my life,
I wouldn't enjoy writing romance.

Whether you've loved
or lost, it's always
worth it!
♡
XOXO,
Crystal Jay

TABLE OF CONTENTS

Magazine Dreams

2017, Present day

"I NEVER SHOULD'VE MARRIED."

Mary stopped playing with the loose thread on the couch and stared at Daniel, replaying the words he'd just said. "Is that why you lost *three* of your wedding rings?"

Daniel opened his mouth and shut it then slumped back against the blue recliner. His gray, greasy hair lay matted across his wrinkled forehead. He looked down at his trembling hands, blinking away the moisture in his red-rimmed eyes.

She shifted on the couch, crossing her arms. "Why would you even say that to me?"

"Because it's true," he said in a quiet tone.

"Well, it's a little late for that. Don't you think?"

He reached for the coffee mug on the end table, taking a long drink.

Mary glanced out the window overlooking the

well-manicured lawn at Pleasant Creek Nursing Home. She couldn't watch him take a drink, knowing there was probably alcohol mixed in it. If only the caretakers at Pleasant Creek could go through his cabinets and throw away all of his bottles. But he lived in an independent apartment, so he had the right to have alcohol in his new home.

Daniel set the mug back on the end table with a thud, getting her attention. "I'm sorry. I really am."

She grunted. "Sorry for what? For marrying me when you shouldn't have? For drinking your way through our marriage?"

His Adam's apple bobbed up and down, and for the first time since she arrived, he met her gaze. "For all of it."

"Your apologies don't cut it anymore. I just want answers." She touched her bare ring finger, knowing answers were all he had left to give her. Two years ago, they'd signed the divorce papers, ending 23 years of marriage.

He pulled himself out of the recliner and trudged toward the kitchen with his mug in hand. His shoulders hunched forward, making him appear at least ten years older and several inches shorter. He refilled his coffee mug and turned around to face her, leaning his hip against the counter. "What do you want to know?"

"Why didn't you come to the bedroom for all those years?"

He lifted the mug to his lips and steam spiraled around his face. "Probably cause I was drinking."

Mary formed a fist, her fingernails biting into her palm. She should have known. It always came back to alcohol. Losing the will to ask anything else, she pulled her purse onto her lap. She might as well get down to business. She grabbed a folder full of Daniel's most recent bills. As his power of attorney, she needed to address his finances.

She took out a credit card statement. "You spent three thousand dollars during your last payment period. That's a thousand dollars over budget."

"I had to buy furniture for this place. All of our stuff is still at the house."

Mary pursed her lips, trying to decide what to say so she didn't start an argument. "It looks like most of your expenses came from Jewell and Walgreens, though."

The mug shook in his trembling hand. "Just pay the bill, please." He said it so quietly she almost didn't hear him.

"Okay."

"Thank you." Daniel walked back into the living room and sat down beside her on the couch. The moisture returned to his glassy eyes as he put a hand on her knee. "I just want you to know I've changed."

A lump formed in her throat. She wanted to believe Daniel, but his credit card statement didn't lie. He was probably buying alcohol at Jewell and Walgreens.

She pinched the bridge of her nose, feeling a headache coming on. "Don't do this."

"But I have. Living by myself, I've had a lot of time to think. I messed up, and I want to make things right."

"How?"

He ran a hand over his five o'clock shadow, seeming to consider her question. "I'll go back to rehab. You can go with me and see my progress."

His voice was drenched in desperation, further shattering the already broken pieces of her heart. "You just told me we shouldn't have gotten married, and now you're saying you want to get married again. You're not making sense."

Daniel put his hand on her cheek. "Back then, I

shouldn't have. I'm a better man, now. I promise."

Her chest constricted. She'd been waiting for him to say those words for years. A part of her hoped that he could change, that they could get remarried, and start over again.

But warning lights flashed across her brain, causing her to remain cautious. How could she ever trust him again?

1989, 28 years earlier …

MARY OPENED THE *Chicago Tribune*, her breath catching in her throat. Her spoon clattered against her bowl of Cheerios, forgotten. She brought the paper closer to her face, eyeing an image of the new wing just added to a treatment and rehabilitation center. A large bow was tied around a sign in the yard of the nursing home, and a man stood next to it with a pair of big scissors spread wide around the bow.

The man had deep-set eyes and dark brown hair, with speckles of gray. He wore a black suit that fit snugly over his lean shoulders, and a tie that made him appear professional.

Whoa. Who was this guy?

She glanced at the article beside the picture, devouring its contents. His name was Daniel Regan. He was an administrator at the nursing home, and it had been his idea to add the new wing to make room for a computer lab, specifically designed for people with disabilities.

Mary put a hand over her chest. Daniel was good looking and he had a big heart for people. What a sweet guy.

She peered hard at the picture again. Did he have a wedding ring on? With his hands holding the scissors, it was hard to tell. She chewed on the inside of her cheek. He had to be older than her if he had gray hair. But now that she was in her thirties, did age really matter?

Not if she found the right person. She'd met enough Mr. Wrongs to know age wasn't a determining factor. And she'd never had such a strong visceral reaction to a picture. That had to mean something.

She laid the newspaper on her kitchen table and drummed her manicured nails against the polished wood. If she could just meet Daniel, then she'd know if she had a chance. But how?

A small advertisement beside the article caught her eye. She leaned forward to read it. The nursing home had an opening for a Therapeutic Recreation Specialist. She almost laughed. *No way.*

She reached for her purse, swinging it over her shoulder. Time to go shopping for a new outfit. She had to look good for her possible interview.

1989, Two months later …

MARY STRODE ACROSS THE COMMON ROOM of Pembroke Nursing Home, her heels click-clacking against the linoleum floor. The assistants wheeled the last few residents into the spacious common room. Most of them stared in her direction, waiting for the show to start.

She reached for the microphone, excitement bubbling in her chest. This was it. Their first performance as Music on Wheels.

Daniel stopped next to her, addressing the small band behind them. "Are you guys ready?"

Two of the band members bobbed their heads

up and down, accidentally shaking their tambourines against the armrests of their wheelchairs.
Another band member laughed at her friends so
loud Mary could barely hear the jingling bells
attached to the woman's shoelaces.

"You'll be great. Just remember: Mary and I
believe in you." Daniel winked at her, his dark blue-
green eyes sparkling beneath the bright fluorescent
lights.

Mary swallowed hard, her whole body reacting
to Daniel's affection. She still couldn't believe she'd
been offered the job at the treatment and rehabilitation center, and she'd spent the last two months
working under Daniel's administration. He was even
more handsome in person, despite being nineteen
years older than her.

But it wasn't just his looks. He had such a kind
heart for helping people with disabilities.

And he was single.

The best part, though, was when he'd discovered
her passion for singing, and he asked if she'd be
interested in starting a music group for people in
wheelchairs. How could she say no to that?
Spending more time with him and starting a singing
group was a no-brainer.

Daniel ran a hand over his sweater vest. He stood so close she could smell the minty gum on his breath. "Let's get this party started," he said.

Nodding, Mary squared her shoulders and tapped her foot. "A one, two, three." She put her hand against her stomach, looking out at the crowd. "Somewhere out there, beneath the pale moonlight ..."

Daniel joined in, his rich tenor blending with her melodic soprano. Behind them, the tambourines started jingling softly, followed by the chiming bells. As the instruments grew louder, she took a few steps closer to the crowd, her arm outstretched. "Someone's thinking of me and loving me tonight."

She glanced at Daniel out of the corner of her eye. Did he see potential for love between them? She'd been looking for someone like him for a long time. He was hardworking, passionate, and well-established. Everything she wanted in a husband.

But he hadn't asked her on a date yet. What was holding him back? His first marriage had ended years ago, so he might still have emotional scars from it. Or maybe he just didn't think they were a good fit. The thought made her chest tighten.

Daniel met her gaze, sending her a warm smile.

His voice grew louder. "Somewhere out there if love can see us through, then we'll be together somewhere out there, out where dreams come true."

Heat crept into her cheeks, and she couldn't look away as they finished the song. The residents clapped politely. Daniel reached for her hand and raised it above their heads before they bowed.

She glanced back at their band. All twelve faces grinned at her. The song hadn't been perfect, but they were pretty good. All those hours of practice had been worth it just to see their smiles. Her heart swelled with pride.

Daniel squeezed her hand. "That was great. We should go out tonight and celebrate."

Her head shot in his direction, but she quickly recovered and tucked a strand of hair behind her ear. "Oh, sure. That sounds like fun."

1992, Three years later …

STANDING IN THE MIDDLE OF the parking lot, Mary tugged at the collar of her pink blouse, airing it out. She let go of her shirt, the reflection of her engagement ring glistening in the sunlight. "I still don't understand why we're here."

Daniel stepped closer to the outpatient center. "I already told you, I want to admit myself."

She bit her lip. "I know that, but is there something else going on that you're not telling me? You're not an alcoholic."

Daniel lowered his chin to his chest, running a hand over his face. "But I am, and I need help." His voice sounded thick, like something had caught in his throat.

Her stomach coiled. She hated seeing him so defeated. Something was definitely wrong, but she still didn't believe it could be alcohol related.

If he really was an alcoholic, she would know. Over the last three years, they'd spent a lot of time together—karaoke on weekends, traveling to county events with Music on Wheels, dinners in downtown Chicago, vacationing in Hawaii. They often drank and sometimes Daniel had a bit too much, but he was laughing and goofing around, the life of the party.

And yet, if he wanted to admit himself into the treatment center, then she would be supportive. She walked toward him, kissing his cheek. "Let's go."

"Thank you." He expelled a breath, smelling like his mint-fresh gum. "I'm so lucky to have you."

She lifted his chin to meet her gaze. "We can get through anything, okay?"

He blinked rapidly then closed his eyes, kissing her with a sense of desperation. She melted into him, parting her lips. She poured all of her love into the kiss, showing him everything she couldn't say in words.

Hopefully, after today, she would get some answers. The staff would probably tell her that Daniel was overreacting, worried about becoming an alcoholic like his dad. If that was the case, they could leave this day behind them and start their promising life together. After all, their wedding was only a month away.

2015, 23 years later …

Mary stared out the window in the entryway of her silent two-story home. Daniel was passed out in the upstairs guest bedroom and wouldn't wake up for hours. Not after coming home at two in the morning. Most nights, she barely heard him when he came home, but last night, he'd walked into the neighbors' house, thinking it was theirs. Thankfully, the neighbors had called her right away instead of calling the cops.

Her head throbbed. She rubbed her temples, trying to ease the pressure. She should go into the kitchen and get ibuprofen, but then she'd have to walk past the stack of bills on the table—bills that Daniel had forgotten to pay, plus the letter from the investment company notifying them that their balance had dropped from $500,000 to $70,000.

So much for a relaxing retirement. Part of her was still furious; part of her had stopped caring. The less she cared, the less pain she felt.

If only she had listened to the counselor at the treatment center all those years ago. After Daniel had admitted himself, the counselor called her back into a private room. The woman told Mary she was in denial, that Daniel really was an alcoholic. Somehow, Mary had still walked out of the treatment center believing Daniel was fine.

She opened the front door and stepped outside, the concrete steps cool beneath her bare feet. She'd thought a lot about their marriage lately, and how well Daniel had hidden his addiction. He'd convinced her to get a second home in Las Vegas. She lived there for several months out of the year, while he lived back in Illinois. So they'd spent a lot of time apart. When they had lived together, he didn't drink in front of her.

But he couldn't hide it anymore. The late nights, the hangovers, the unpaid bills, his slipping memory—it was all adding up. She'd convinced him to go back to treatment, and he would go for a few days, then leave and go right back to drinking.

Mary slumped down on the steps, covering her head in her hands. *What was she supposed to do?* She loved Daniel, and she ached to be there for him like she'd promised. But he wouldn't listen to her. He was out of control, and she was helpless.

Hot tears slipped down her cheeks. No matter what she decided to do, she'd already lost her husband.

2017, Present day

MARY SHIFTED ON THE COUCH and Daniel dropped

his hand away from her cheek. She slipped his financial records back into her purse, replaying his words. *I've changed. I'm a better man.*

Daniel expelled a deep breath. "You don't believe me, do you?"

She ran her finger along the strap of her purse. "I'm not sure what to believe about you. But I do know this . . ." She glanced up, meeting his gaze. "I've had enough. I can't do it anymore."

His bushy eyebrows furrowed together, and he slumped back against the couch. "Okay."

"Okay?"

"Yeah. That's not what I want to hear, but I get it."

She turned toward him and put her hand on his shoulder. "I will always love you, and I'm so glad we could stay friends through all of this." She paused for a moment, collecting her thoughts. "I know I'm hard on you sometimes when I visit, and I'm sorry. It's just … I wish things could've been different, you know?"

Daniel ran a hand over his five o'clock shadow. "Me too."

"Come here." Mary pulled him closer, slipping her arms around his neck. She rested her chin on his shoulder and squeezed her eyes shut. No matter what, she would be there for him—maybe not in the way she'd imagined, but she would always care about Daniel.

WHERE ARE THEY NOW?

DANIEL LIVES IN AN INDEPENDENT living apartment. He was recently diagnosed with Alcohol Dementia. Mary goes to Al-Anon meetings, a support group for friends and family members of alcoholics. She often speaks and shares her story to let others know they are not alone.

Mary moved to Iowa to be closer to her family. Sometimes she's lonely, but she enjoys spending time with her family and meeting new people. She's ready to meet a man she can spend the rest of her life with.

Uncharted Territory

Tony

Ten Years Old (1971)

TONY LISTON DASHED ACROSS THE living room, his short, small frame weaving between large cardboard boxes and furniture scattered across the dusty hardwood floor. He turned around and took a couple of steps back, searching for his younger brother among all the other kids.

Tim's dark hair appeared above a pile of boxes labeled *kitchen*.

"Go long." Tony threw the football, and as it spiraled through the air, Tim ran backward, keeping his eye on the ball. As it neared, Tim jumped and lunged to the side. The ball shot right past his outstretched arms, smacking into his tiny chest with a light thud. He wrapped his arms around the ball and ran right into a box. It toppled over, and pots and pans slid onto the floor, their metal handles clattering against the hardwood.

Tony smacked his forehead. *Come on, Tim.* If his brother had broken anything, he'd get them both into trouble.

Tim jumped up, clutching the ball in his hand and extending his arm in the air, mimicking Mean Joe Green after making a touchdown.

Tony smirked. At least his brother had good taste. "Nice catch."

"What was that noise?" Mom's voice came from the foyer. Her tone was drenched with irritation.

He pushed his coke-bottle glasses to the top of his nose and heat crept up the back of his neck. They didn't normally play ball in the house, but he'd been trying to keep his younger brothers and all the other kids occupied. As soon as their moving truck had pulled up in front of the parsonage, families had been in and out of their house, welcoming them to town. The best way to keep the little ones out of his parents' way was to play catch. Or so he'd thought.

His mom appeared in the doorway, her arms crossed above her plaid button-down shirt. Stepping into the living room, her gaze traveled to the pots and pans on the floor. A low *tsk* noise escaped through her pursed lips, and a look of disappointment flashed across her face. "Please don't make a mess."

His shoulders lowered. "Sorry. I'll pick it up."

"Thank you." She uncrossed her arms and pointed at the football. "No more ball in the house. The rules haven't changed. They're the same ones we've always had."

"Okay."

She shook her head and went to check on the baby.

Tony kneeled down on the floor. Picking up a large pot, he set it back inside the box. He hated disappointing his mom. As the oldest, he felt like he had to be the responsible one, if only to make her life easier.

Too bad Mom or Dad didn't care about making *his* life easier. In fact, when Dad accepted the head pastorate position for First Christian Church, it felt like he had single-handedly ruined Tony's life. He wouldn't complain about it, though. Mom and Dad were convinced the Lord wanted them to serve in this new place. He was trying to see it that way too, but it wasn't easy.

All his friends lived in Paoli, Indiana, two hours

away. He would never see them again. Plus, they'd moved a month into the school year. And not just any school year—fifth grade. It would've been the best year ever. It was one of the highest grades at his old elementary, so he had been the top dog at school. All those younger kids had looked up to him, just like he'd looked up to the fifth and sixth graders last year.

But here in Brazil, Indiana no one would know him. The new elementary was much bigger than his old school. Would anyone even notice him? He'd had the same friends since he was a little boy, so making new friends was uncharted territory.

Setting another pan in the box, he expelled a heavy breath. Somehow, he'd have to find positive reasons for living in Brazil. It was the right thing to do.

Three quick knocks rapped on the front door. He jumped up and dashed to the living room window, pulling back the drapes. It was probably another family from the church, welcoming them to the neighborhood.

The doorbell rang, sending a long, shrill melody above the noisy chaos inside the house. He pulled the drapes back farther. A blond-haired girl stood on the stoop, wearing a denim dress with embroidered flowers. She looked about the same height as him. Maybe they were in the same grade. So far all the kids who'd stopped by were much younger or older.

From the foyer, Mom cleared her throat, glancing in his direction. "Stop peeking through the window," she whispered. She opened the door and turned her attention to the new visitors.

He dashed to her side, stopping in his tracks. The girl was super cute. Her golden blond hair cascaded past her shoulders, stopping just below her tiny waist. With her long hair and light brown freckles sprinkled across her nose and cheeks, she looked like a younger version of Marcia Brady.

"Hi." A slow, shy smile spread across her face. She adjusted the pie in her hands, clutching it closer to her stomach. Her big hazel eyes stared at him expectantly, and he realized she was waiting for him to respond.

"Um, hi." Tony pushed his glasses up higher on his nose, and then jammed his hands in his pockets. Too bad he hadn't brought the football with him. He would've looked a lot groovier.

A woman appeared beside the girl, her heels clicking against the cement porch. He forced his gaze away from the girl to look at the woman. She shook hands with his mom. "I'm Joyce, and this is my daughter, Stephenie."

"Nice to meet both of you." Mom stepped back and ushered the ladies into the foyer. Their moms made small talk, and he stopped paying attention. He couldn't focus. Not with this pretty girl standing right in front of him.

Still mesmerized by her resemblance to Marcia Brady, he tried not to stare. His gaze traveled to the pie in her hands. "Is that for us?"

She nodded. "I made it with my mom. It's apple."

"Yum."

"Do you want it?" She lifted the pie tin, holding it above her outstretched arms.

"Oh. Yeah." He took his hands out of his pockets and reached for the pie. For a brief moment, his hand brushed against hers. Her skin felt soft and velvety, sending his heart racing.

He set the pie on the steps behind him and leaned against the wooden railing of the grand staircase. "So, what grade are you in?"

"Third. You?"

"Fifth."

Her eyes widened and he lifted his chin a bit higher, satisfied that he'd impressed her. On second thought, maybe she was surprised, assuming he was younger. His shoulders wilted. If only he were taller.

Stephenie lowered her gaze, her attention falling on the white bassinet beside him. "Is that a baby in there?"

"Yeah. That's my littlest brother." Tony pulled back the top cover, revealing a baby with big round cheeks and dark curly hair. The baby stirred, moving a tiny curled fist up by his mouth.

"Aw, he's so cute. How many brothers and sisters do you have?"

"Four brothers." He gently pulled the cover back over the bassinet, trying not to wake Andrew. "What about you?"

"It's just me." She stared down at her hands. "It must be fun to have such a big family."

He nodded. "But you can borrow my brothers anytime you want."

Stephenie laughed. "I don't think it works that way."

"You can't say I didn't offer."

"That's true." Stephenie played with the hem of her dress, twirling a loose thread around her finger.

He pushed off the wall, puffing his chest out a little. He had to say something else to impress her. "Want to know something really cool?"

"Yes …"

"This morning, I found a secret stairway leading up to the second floor."

She put a hand over her mouth, a disbelieving look filling her big hazel eyes. "No way."

"Uh-huh. Wanna see it?"

Stephenie tugged on her mom's dress, her eyes lighting with excitement. "Can I go see inside?"

Her mom glanced down at her watch. "Not today, sweetie. We've intruded long enough. They need to finish unpacking."

Stephenie crossed her arms, pouting. "Please?"

"Maybe another time." Her mom exchanged a look with his parents. "If the Liston's invite us back, of course."

Mom put a hand on his shoulder, squeezing it. "We'd love to have Stephenie over to play some- time. Wouldn't we, Tony?"

Resisting the urge to scream *yes,* Tony shrugged. "Sure." He couldn't act too eager, especially in front of a third grader. He didn't want to look desperate for friends.

Stephenie smiled. "Sweet. I'll catch ya on the flip side, then." Tossing her hair behind her shoulder, she turned around and walked outside with her mom.

Tony stood a little taller. Stephenie was one groovy chic. Maybe moving to Brazil wouldn't be so bad after all.

Tony

Sixteen Years Old (1977)

TONY STOOD OUTSIDE THE STARK, white hospital room and smoothed his hair. He'd been growing it out over the last few months, trying to look more like John Travolta. With just the right amount of hair gel, he was getting close.

He stepped inside and stuffed his hands inside the pocket of his sweatshirt. Across the room, Stephenie slept in the bed. Her long hair splayed out across the sheets, tucked neatly beneath her thin arms. Her eyes were closed, her long lashes gracing her pale cheeks. She looked like Sleeping Beauty.

He tiptoed across the room, not wanting to

wake her. She was probably tired and sore from surgery. He set a chair beside her bed and sat down, glancing at the TV. On the screen, Fonzie stood beside a booth at Al's Diner, talking to Richie Cunningham. Fonzie snapped his fingers, and a blond bombshell walked up to his side, looping her arm around his waist, just below his brown leather jacket. "Aaaaayy," Fonzie said, smirking at the girl. "Let's get outta here."

That was exactly what he wanted to say to Stephenie. It didn't seem right to see her lying in a hospital bed with a brace around her neck. But hopefully the surgery helped straighten her spine.

She mumbled something incoherent, and he stood up next to her bed. With the brace holding her neck in place, she probably couldn't see him sitting down. "Hey."

Her eyes fluttered open, then shut, and open again. She stared at him for a moment as if she couldn't decide if he was real or not. "What are you doing here?"

"What does it look like I'm doing? I'm visiting you."

She blinked again, glancing behind him out the window. Snow spiraled through the air, so quickly the ground was barely visible. "I thought the interstates were closed down. My parents couldn't even visit me today. How did you get here?"

"My dad took the back roads."

"He's such a great guy. It's really sweet that he keeps coming to see me." Her voice sounded low and groggy, probably from all the pain medication. "Where is he?"

"Grabbing a coffee downstairs. He'll be up soon." Tony rocked back on his heels. Hopefully, she wasn't disappointed it was just him for now.

"So, are you doing some kind of pastor training?"

His eyebrows furrowed together. "Training?"

"Don't you want to be a pastor someday?"

"Yeah, but—"

"Is that why you're here? To practice visiting people at the hospital?"

"Not really. I figured I'd check out the big city. I've never been to Indianapolis before." He glanced out the window for a moment, unable to meet her eyes as he spoke. What he said was only partially true. He'd mostly come to see her.

Not that he would tell her that. Over the last several years, they'd seen each other at school and church, but they'd barely spoken. With two grade levels between them, they didn't have many opportunities to talk. So when his dad had mentioned visiting Stephenie, he knew he had to go. He couldn't give up a chance to talk to her. "So … how's your back?"

She gave him a somber look. "The doctor isn't sure if the surgery worked. I might be hunch-backed in a few years."

"For real?"

Stephenie laughed. "You really believed me?"

"Of course not. I was just humoring you."

"Oh yeah? Then why did your eyes bug out of your head?"

"No comment."

"Actually, the surgery went really well." She went on to tell him all about her surgery and the two steel rods holding her spine in place, using medical jargon throughout her explanation.

He listened intently, nodding and pretending he understood everything she was saying. Stephenie was so smart. It made her appear older than she really was. If only it were true, they could have more opportunities to hang out.

"How long are you stuck in here?" he asked

when she was finished.

She sighed. "Two months."

"At least you get to miss school."

"I know. I'll actually miss the rest of the year. My parents hired a tutor."

"You're lucky."

"Tell me about it. How's school going for you?"

He shrugged. "Same old, same old. Homecoming's next weekend."

"Are you going with anyone?"

"Yeah. I asked Marilyn."

"Oh." Stephenie picked at her thumbnail, chipping away at the polish. Flecks of blue landed on the white sheet. "Are you going steady?"

"No. We've only gone on a few dates." Tony smirked. "Why? Are you jealous, Stephenie?" he pestered.

"Humph. Please." She rolled her eyes. "And you can call me Steph. That's what my friends have started calling me."

"Sheesh, *Steph*, I'm not that bad." He rested his hip against the bed. "At least, Marilyn doesn't think so. She says I'm foxy."

Steph gave him a coy smile, keeping her voice smooth and steady. "Looks aren't everything, you know."

He kept a straight face, but Steph's words made his chest pinch with disappointment. Did that mean she didn't find him attractive? And why did he suddenly feel disappointed? He stepped back from the bed, putting more space between them so he could think clearly. It had to be a fluke reaction.

While there was no denying how pretty she was, Steph would never be anything more than a family friend. Plus, she was too young to date a high school boy like himself.

Stephenie

Sixteen Years Old (1979)

STEPHENIE THOMAS STOOD IN FRONT of the youth group, her hands shaking as she held the monologue in front of her. Over the rim of the paper, twenty eyes stared in her direction.

Heat flamed beneath her cheeks. How had Tony Liston talked her into this? He was the youth ministry intern now, so when he'd asked her to play Ruth, she couldn't tell him no.

Get it together, Steph. Everyone's waiting for you. Squaring her shoulders, she looked down at the paper and started reading. All of her prepared words tumbled out of her mouth. By the time she was done a few minutes later, she expelled a relieved breath. Thank God it was over.

The youth group clapped, and she sat back down at a table near the back of the small room. Dawn took her place on the makeshift stage, reading the Queen Esther monologue with confident eloquence.

Steph crossed her arms. Too bad Tony hadn't asked *her* to play Queen Esther. At least she could've felt better about being the beautiful queen compared to the young widow. Tony obviously thought Dawn was better suited to be the beautiful one. Dawn *did* look like Barbie. Not that it really mattered. It wasn't like she cared what the pastor's son thought about her.

Dawn finished her monologue and the youth group clapped wildly. Steph sunk down in her seat. Maybe she should've practiced more.

Tony stood and addressed the group. "That was a lot of fun. Let's wrap up with a prayer. Does anyone have any prayer requests?" He listened as several people raised their hands, asking for prayers regarding sick grandparents, grades, and rocky relationships with parents. When no one else raised a hand, he bowed his head and led the group in prayer.

Steph closed her eyes and tried to focus on Tony's slow, calming tone instead of all the negative thoughts eating away at her confidence. He had the perfect pastor's voice: he knew just when to raise his voice excitedly and when to sound serious, making each word resonate deep within you. It made his lessons engaging and his prayers meaningful. Any church would be lucky to have him as a pastor one day.

"Amen."

Steph opened her eyes as Tony raised his head. His gaze met hers across the room. He weaved through the chairs in the room, stopping in front of her. A proud smile spread across his face. "That was really good, Steph."

"Yeah right." She folded the paper in half, running her thumb along the crease. "You're just saying that because you asked me to read one of the monologues."

"That's not true. I thought you conveyed Ruth

perfectly."

She glanced up from the folded paper. "Really?"

"Yes." He sat down next to her, crossing a leg over his knee. "Can I tell you something?"

"What?"

"Ruth is one of my favorite women in the Bible."

"She is?"

Tony chuckled. "Man, you're questioning everything I say. I didn't know I was that full of surprises."

"No, it's not that …" She wasn't about to tell him she'd wanted to be Esther instead. Obviously, she'd misread Tony's choices for the monologues. "Never mind."

"Okay." Tony pushed his glasses higher on his nose. "Anyway, Ruth is awesome because she's such a good friend to Naomi. I mean, she left everything she knew to follow Naomi to a different land. Can you imagine doing that for someone?"

Steph shook her head and lifted her chin a little higher. Wow, Tony not only liked Ruth, but he admired her. And he'd chosen *her* to be Ruth. This situation was getting better and better. Unless … A seed of doubt sprouted, taking root inside her brain.

Maybe she'd been so terrible that he was just trying to make her feel better.

Why did she always have to doubt herself? She looked at Tony, trying to decide which reasoning made the most sense.

Before she could make a decision, Tony continued. "That's why I think you played Ruth so well. You're a good friend to people."

"Oh, um thanks." So he'd really meant it. The thought left a pleasing sensation traveling through her stomach, light and airy like jumping on a trampoline.

Whoa. Where had that feeling come from? This was Tony, after all. The pastor's son. This was her mom's fault. Just last week she'd asked, *Why don't you date that Tony Liston boy?* Her response at the time had been easy. *Because he has a girlfriend.* But now that he was sitting here making her feel better, she allowed herself to wonder about the possibility. If he didn't have a girlfriend, would she be interested?

He'd always been nice to her, from that very first day he'd offered to show her the secret stairway in his house to the day he'd visited her at the hospital. But she'd never imagined being more than friends with him.

Why was she even questioning this? It didn't matter. He *did* have a girlfriend. And he was going to college in the fall. A college guy would never consider dating a girl in high school.

Stephenie
Seventeen Years Old (1980)

"STEPHIE, THE PHONE'S FOR YOU!" Her mom's voice carried from the kitchen.

Steph leaned over her bed, reaching for the phone on her nightstand. A stack of magazines slid across her comforter, piling near her crossed legs. "Hello?"

"Hey Steph."

Her heart skipped a beat. "Oh, hi."

Terry, who was sitting next to her on the bed, stopped flipping through the latest issue of *Teen* and gave her a questioning look.

Steph cupped her hand over the receiver. "It's Tony Liston." She sent an I-have-no-idea-why-he'd-be-calling-me look back at her friend. She hadn't seen him since he'd left for college last year.

Terry waved her hand, reminding Steph to say something to Tony. "What's up?"

"You know Florence from church?"

"Yeah. Why?"

"She's taking a bunch of the people from youth group out to dinner on Friday night, and I was wondering if you'd be my date."

A flush of adrenaline tingled through her body. His date? Did that mean he liked her? *Wait.* What had happened to his girlfriend?

She chewed on the inside of her cheek, new worries emerging. She'd gone on dates before, but she'd never dated anyone seriously. Not like Tony, who'd dated the same girl throughout high school. He had much more experience than she did.

"Say something," Terry whispered.

"Okay, I'll go."

"Great. I'll pick you up at six."

She hung up the phone and covered her face with her hands. "I can't believe that just happened."

Terry twisted a short strand of brown hair around her finger. "I should tell you something."

"What is it?" Steph dropped her hands, clasping them in her lap.

"Tony already asked Debbie, and she couldn't go."

"I was just an afterthought, then." Steph flopped back against her pillow, her heart pounding in her chest. "He doesn't like me. I should've said no too."

"Do you want him to like you?"

"I don't know. Maybe." She sat back up, meeting Terry's gaze. "You go instead."

"No way. He didn't ask me. I bet Dawn is going with Tim. Maybe you could all go together, since they're brothers and all."

Her spirits lifted a little. Terry was probably right. Dawn and Tim had been dating for the last year and they were always hanging out. "It wouldn't be so bad if Dawn was there."

"See, it'll be fine. And he could like you. Maybe he was just scared to ask you first."

"Yeah right," Steph mumbled. Terry was just trying to make her feel better. And yet, what if her friend was right? A glimmer of hope lifted her spirits. She'd have to look for a sign, something to show her that he actually liked her.

Gaining a new resolve, her gaze traveled toward the closet. "Want to help me pick out a cute outfit?" She had to look good, just in case.

Tony

Nineteen Years Old (1980)

TONY STOOD IN THE CROWDED LOBBY of the restaurant, waiting to be seated and shifting his weight from one foot to the other. He put his hands in his pockets, only to take them out a minute later. Beads of sweat trickled down his back. He adjusted his tie to give him more room to breathe and aired out his button-down shirt. He readjusted his tie, making it tighter. With Steph standing beside him, he needed to look calm and composed.

He'd never seen Steph so dressed up before. She looked beautiful, wearing a knee-length denim dress and tall brown boots. He couldn't keep his eyes off of her.

Florence lifted her cane in the air, waiting for the youth group to quiet down. While she waited to get everyone's attention, she lowered her cane and peered at the group through her up-turned, diamond-studded glasses. "Ladies and gentlemen, we can be seated now. I paid for the buffet, so once you get to the table, go ahead and fill your plates."

In front of him, Tim, Dawn, and several other youth group kids thanked Florence.

Smiling, she turned around and inched toward the back of the restaurant, looking over her shoulder to make sure the youth group was following her. Tony smirked. Florence would be a hard lady to lose: her thick fur coat stood out in stark contrast to the light summer jackets everyone else was wearing.

Walking side by side, Steph glanced over at him. "Florence cracks me up."

"You can say that again. She was adamant that everyone had a date tonight, and I have no idea why. I tried asking her, but she just stared at me." Tony laughed, shaking his head.

Steph didn't seem as amused. She bit her bottom lip. "So you didn't want to bring a date?"

"No, it's not that. It's ..." He sighed, knowing he should be honest with her. "Marilyn just broke up with me."

"Oh." Her eyes filled with compassion. "I'm sorry to hear that. You guys went steady for a long time."

Tony shrugged. "I'm fine. It was for the best, but I didn't feel ready to go on a date yet." He paused for a moment, realizing he'd probably said too much. He needed to turn this conversation around.

He nudged her shoulder with his. "But then you said you'd be my date, and I was glad for Florence's crazy rule."

Stopping midstride, Steph gave him a hard look as if she was trying to decide if she believed him.

Bummer. Somehow, he'd given her a reason to question him. Was it the recent break up or how he'd mentioned not wanting to bring a date? Before he could think about it for too long, Steph walked the last few feet to the table and picked up her plate. "Let's go get some food."

Nodding, he followed her to the buffet. This was not how he'd imagined the date going. Ever since he was a little boy, he'd thought so highly of Steph. She'd always been too young to date, but now she was a senior in high school. She was almost a legal adult.

He'd still been hesitant to ask her to dinner though. So he'd asked Debbie instead, thinking they could go as friends. But when she'd said no, Steph immediately came to mind. After all, he could only come up with so many excuses. And when she'd said yes, he'd let out a little whoop.

"Ew, gross." Steph pointed to a container in the middle of the buffet, scrunching her nose. "Pickled herring."

Tony stopped right beside her, their arms almost touching. "That looks disgusting."

A slow grin spread across her face, a mischievous twinkle sparkling in her eyes. "I dare you to try it."

He shook his head. "Uh-uh."

"Come on, you know you want to." She laid her hand on his forearm.

Every hair on his arm stood on end from her touch. He glanced up, meeting her gaze. If eating pickled herring was what it took to show Steph he liked her, then so be it. "Okay, fine. I'll try it."

She giggled. "Seriously?"

"Yup." Grabbing a ladle, he scooped up a big helping, trying not to inhale the fishy smell. He picked up a small piece with his fingers and tossed it in his mouth.

"I can't believe you're actually eating it." Steph scrunched her nose again, looking so adorably cute he grabbed another piece and swallowed it quickly.

"Satisfied?" he asked.

"You bet." Her cheeks turned crimson as they exchanged a long glance. The doubt in her eyes was gone, replaced with something else entirely … attraction.

His heart picked up speed, pounding so hard he wondered if she could hear it. He wasn't ashamed if she could. After all these years of tucking away his feelings, it felt freeing to embrace them.

Tony
One month later …

TONY DROVE DOWN STEPH'S STREET, stopping his 1976 Chevette in front of her house. The sun disappeared below the horizon, and the streetlamp turned on above them. In the semi-darkness, the lamp created a hazy luminescence behind Steph's open passenger window, casting an ethereal glow on her skin.

She rested her arm on the window frame and turned toward him. "That was a really good lesson."

"I added too much personal information."

"No, you didn't. You made it really relevant." She gave him a playful shove. "Don't be so hard on yourself."

He smiled. "I'll try not to."

"I can't believe your internship is almost over."

"I know. It's gone by fast." Staring into her eyes, fun couldn't even begin to describe how much the time with Steph had meant to him. After Florence's dinner, they'd spent almost every day together. Walking around the mall, canoeing, putt-putting with the youth group, hanging out at his house for pizza on Friday nights. As an intern for the youth group, he'd even given Steph a leadership role so he'd be able to see her more often.

She played with a loose thread on her plaid capris, her face turning somber.

"Is something wrong?" He twisted a dial on the dashboard, lowering the volume.

"I've had a lot of fun with you this summer. I don't want it to be over."

He reached for her hand, drawing circles on her palm. "Me either. You mean a lot to me."

Saying the words out loud made his heart squeeze. They'd only been dating two months, but going steady with Steph wasn't the typical situation. He didn't need time to fall in love with her. He was already in love with her. And now he was so deep in love, he couldn't imagine why it had taken him so long to ask her out.

"You mean a lot to me, too." Looking down at their hands, Steph twisted her lips. "But where is this going?"

His mouth went dry. He felt so sure about his future with Steph, but that didn't mean she felt the same way. Next year, she would attend Oral Roberts University to become a surgeon. They weren't exactly taking the same paths in life.

He let go of her hand and tucked a golden lock behind her ear. If he didn't tell her how he felt, he would always wonder what could have been. "Anyone I might marry someday would have to be a lot like you. In fact, exactly like you." Staring into her eyes, he brought his face inches away from hers. "So if you're okay with it, I'd rather just date you and no one else."

"I'd like that." A big grin spread across her face, her eyes confirming what he'd hoped to see—that she loved him too.

With his heart beating wildly in his chest, Tony rested his elbow on the console, his gaze lingering on her lips. She inched closer, her chest rising and falling as she closed her eyes. Crossing the distance, he pressed his lips against hers. Heat radiated from his lips to his toes. Fireworks shot off inside his stomach, like when Millicent kissed Bobby Brady for the first time.

This wasn't the first time he'd kissed Steph, but after confessing his intentions, this kiss meant so much more. It would be a hard road for the next few years while they were separated, but he knew without a doubt that he would marry Steph one day.

WHERE ARE THEY NOW?

STEPH WAS ONLY AT Oral Roberts University for a couple of days before she told her parents she wanted to attend Ozark Christian College with Tony. She decided to forgo being a surgeon and majored in ministry, knowing that she could still touch many lives.

Tony proposed later that semester. This year, they will celebrate 34 years of marriage. Early in their marriage, Tony and Steph moved to Davenport, Iowa to plant a church, Adventure Christian Community. They have two grown boys and one teenage daughter. They've spent their lives serving God, and they are looking forward to retirement.

BREAKING ALL THE RULES

ANNIE DAVIS PILED HER STACK of cards and turned the top card over, revealing a two of hearts. As soon as she saw the low card, her shoulders drooped. *Dang it.* Why couldn't it have been a king or an ace?

Beside her, Brooke sipped from her beer, sending a sympathetic look over the tipped can. This was the third time Annie had lost a battle. It wouldn't be so bad, but there were consequences in this game.

Annie had just met several of Brooke's new Texas friends, and many of them tapped their red plastic cups against the table. "Shot. Shot. Shot." One of the girls—whose name she couldn't remember—grabbed a thin bottle, unscrewing the red cap.

Bile rose in Annie's throat. "What's that?"

"It's fireball."

"That sounds awful."

The girl smiled mischievously. An hour ago,

when everyone had arrived at the cabin, they'd decided to play drinking games. Brooke had immediately told everyone that Annie didn't drink often. Her best friend had said it so they would go easy on her. But so far, Brooke's friends seemed to have one goal in mind—give her the strongest options they had in stock.

Lucas put his hand over the girl's. "I'll pour it."

Annie met his gaze across the table. She definitely hadn't forgotten *his* name. The moment Lucas Buchanan had walked into the cabin, they'd locked eyes. He had the palest blue eyes she'd ever seen, the kind she could get lost in. Running a hand through his disheveled undercut, he strode across the open space and introduced himself to her in a Southern accent. He had a firm, yet gentle handshake that lingered for a few seconds longer than necessary.

Not that she'd minded. It gave her a few more seconds to admire him from close range. He looked like a surfer with his light-blond beard, athletic shorts, and blue cutoff shirt that showcased his tan, well-defined arms.

And now her fate was in his hands. As the group continued playing, she gave him a look, silently pleading not to give her a shot of fireball. No doubt it would make her sick.

Lucas grabbed a can of root beer, pouring it into her shot glass and sliding it across the table.

She glanced at the others, but no one had noticed. They were laughing at something Brooke had said.

Downing the root beer, she turned back to Lucas, a smile spreading across her face. What a sweet guy for giving her pop instead of alcohol. "Thank you."

"You're welcome. I can be your official shot pourer if you want."

"I'd like that." She twisted the empty shot glass in her hands, trying to focus on something besides the undercurrent of attraction that sparked between them. She'd never been so interested in someone she'd just met. Lucas was practically a stranger.

She needed to be careful. She had just broken up with Owen after dating him for two years. Even though it was for the best, she missed him.

In fact, that was probably the reason Lucas appealed to her. In the morning, she'd wake up and realize it was a fluke. Sudden attraction always fizzled out as quickly as it appeared.

THE NEXT NIGHT, ANNIE TOSSED a log into the fireplace and sat down on the stone hearth, extending her long legs onto the bear fur rug. Heat radiated from the fire, warming her back beneath her thin cotton tank top. Despite the humid summer weather, it didn't seem right to stay in a log cabin without using the fireplace.

Yawning, she cupped a hand over her mouth. She really should go to bed. Only Brooke, Lucas, and a few others were still up, playing drinking games in the basement. Their laughter floated up the staircase.

She reached for her tea, holding the mug with both hands. She couldn't bring herself to go to bed just yet. Her mind was reeling, replaying the events from the day: swimming in the lake, going to Sonic, playing card games. The whole day she'd been so viscerally aware of Lucas it felt like a magnetic pull tugging her closer to him.

Clearly, she'd been wrong about her attraction fizzling out. It had only grown stronger, watching him jump off the dock, swimming laps in the lake, and playing volleyball in the sandpit. He wasn't as outgoing as the rest of the guys here, but his quiet confidence intrigued her.

She wouldn't do anything about it, though. After this week, she'd drive back to Kansas and forget about Lucas in Texas. She'd done long distance before: wishing she could go out to dinner with her boyfriend on weeknights, but ending up on her couch with a box of macaroni instead; spending Friday nights in the car driving to see him; coming home on Sunday nights, only to feel exhausted on Monday; waiting for each phone call just to hear his voice but knowing it would never be as good as spending time in person. No way would she put herself through that again.

The grandfather clock chimed midnight and she startled, spilling a little bit of tea on her leggings. "Crap." She set down the mug and rubbed at the spot with her thumb.

"Are you getting sloppy? I told you not to drink so much."

Annie's head shot up, heat burning in her cheeks as Lucas walked around the fireplace.

He stopped in front of her, shaking his head. "Too much root beer will do that to you."

Annie smiled. "I should've listened to you,

huh?"

Lucas crossed his arms, his chest muscles grow-ing even larger beneath his white V-neck shirt. "I've been told I give pretty good advice."

"Uh-huh, sure. That's what they all say."

He laughed. "Wow, thanks for the vote of con-fidence." He glanced over at her still-full mug, and his face grew somber. "Something keeping you up?"

"Just thinking."

He nodded, seeming to consider her answer, but not pressing her for more. "I'm not in the mood to go to bed either and everyone else just passed out. Want to go out to the dock?"

She rubbed her palms against her legs. She should say no. It would make leaving Texas that much easier, but Lucas was looking at her, his pale blue eyes melting her reasoning into a murky puddle. "Okay. Sure."

Outside, they walked side-by-side, but she was careful to leave a few inches between them. She tried to focus on her surroundings instead. The moon glowed in the star-filled sky, casting a dim light over the dark lake. Down below the dock, frogs croaked, their deep, rhythmic chants competing with the hooting owls and crickets in the nearby woods.

A warm summer breeze blew across the dock, strong enough to pick up Lucas' Calvin Klein cologne, blowing a musky nutmeg scent past her nose.

Ugh. So much for not focusing on him. Even the outdoors noticed Lucas' presence.

He stepped a little closer as they neared the end of the dock, his hand brushing against hers. "Brooke is a lot of fun. She seems to like Texas so far."

"Yeah, she does. I admire her for moving away from everyone she knows and starting a new life here." Annie tossed her hair in front of her shoulder, running her fingers through the long brown strands. "I miss her a lot. We've known each other since we were born. It sucks having her so far away. We talk on the phone all the time, though."

"How far away is Kansas?"

"It's takes about twelve hours to drive. I could fly too, but it's pretty expensive, especially on a youth pastor's salary."

"I should've guessed. Do you like being a pastor?"

"Yeah, and I love the church where I work. It's really big, but it still has this homey, small community vibe. A lot of the families who go to my church are wealthy, so we have the funds to take the kids on mission trips every summer. It's very eye opening for them to see third-world poverty."

"I bet. Where have you gone?"

"New York City and Kenya."

Lucas stopped at the end of the dock, leaning his back against the wooden railing. "I've always wanted to go on a mission trip. But growing up, I could never go with my youth group because they'd go during the summer when I had baseball games."

"You're a baseball player?"

"I played in high school and college. But I don't play much anymore."

Annie rested her forearms above the railing, facing the lake. She liked imagining him in a baseball uniform: tight pants accenting his fit waist, a jersey showcasing his muscular arms, little blond hairs sticking out between his hat and ears. "You could always join an adult league or something."

"I've thought about signing up for a co-ed league. But I need to find someone who would do it with me."

"If I lived closer, I'd do it with you." The second the words came out, she gritted her teeth and pressed her lips together. Had she really just said that? "I mean, don't you have anyone here you could ask?" She wanted to smack her forehead. *Worse, much worse.*

Lucas turned around, facing the same direction as her. A playful smile spread across his face. "Are you asking if I have a girlfriend?"

"No, that's not what I meant. I was just …"

He chuckled. "I'm not seeing anyone."

"Oh." She cracked her knuckles, contemplating how to turn this conversation around to safer, non-relationship related topics.

"Are you dating anyone?"

Annie sighed, giving in. If she told Lucas it was none of his business that would be rude. She might as well answer him. "No. My boyfriend and I just broke up."

"Sorry to hear that." Lucas kept his voice monotone, but his face held little compassion.

"You don't look very sorry."

"Okay, you caught me." He held his hands up in innocence. "I can't help it, though. I've only known you for a couple of days, and already I see what a catch you are."

Annie smiled politely. "Thanks."

"So what happened?"

She swallowed hard. Her wounds were still open and talking about Owen would surely rub them raw. But Lucas looked genuinely interested, and she didn't want to end the conversation. "My ex and I had very different views on faith and politics. For a long time, I tried to convince myself that we could make it work, but in the end ..." Her chest constricted, wishing things could have been different between her and Owen. "I knew it would cause problems in a marriage."

Lucas nodded. "Faith is important to me too. I've always heard that you should date someone who can love God more than you."

She stared at him for a moment, chills running up and down her arms. "My grandpa used to tell me that."

"Your grandpa is a wise man."

"Was." She blinked away the moisture building in her eyes. "He recently passed away."

"I'm sorry to hear that. Like truly sorry this time."

She laughed at his insistence. "My grandpa was a great guy. He's one of the reasons my faith is so strong. He was the pastor of a church and one of those people who befriended everyone. There were over 1,200 people at his funeral."

"Wow. That's when you know someone's touched a lot of lives." Lucas rested his forearms above the railing, his bare skin touching hers. "Is your family doing okay?"

"Yeah, we kind of expected it. He wasn't sick or anything, but my grandma died last year, and he took a turn for the worse after she passed. They were still so in love, even in their late eighties."

"I hope I'll have a love like that one day."

Annie nodded, her heart expanding in her chest. After her grandpa died, she'd yearned to have a deep conversation like this with Owen, but it never happened. Owen was fun to talk to, but he wasn't the type of guy who enjoyed life talks. Lucas, on the other hand, seemed comfortable with them.

As reluctant as she was to start *anything* with Lucas, she couldn't hold back anymore. She wanted to know everything about him. "Have you been in love before?"

"Yeah. I've dated a few people seriously, but the timing never felt right with any of them." He gently ran his fingers over her arm, sending tingles through her body.

"I get that," she said. "I've dated some really

great guys. But so far, nothing has worked out long term. Sometimes I feel so anxious, like it's never going to work out."

"Don't say that. It will. You haven't met the right guy yet." Lucas turned toward her, moonlight casting shadows across his face. "Or maybe you have, and you need to get to know him better."

"You never know …" Suddenly, she felt a little self-conscious, if only because she could guess where this conversation was headed. By the end of the night, they would have to make a decision on what they wanted to do. Would they start dating? A big part of her hoped so, and yet, what if it didn't work out? Long-distance relationships were a big investment and if it ended in heartbreak, it would all be for nothing. It was probably better to stick to her rules and not pursue a long-distance relationship.

Lucas cleared his throat. "What do you look for in someone you date?"

"Oh man, you're putting me on the spot. I would say someone who's a good communicator, someone who shares the same values, and someone who's kind to other people. I'm sure I have more, but that's what comes to mind right away." She tucked a strand of hair behind her ear. "What about you?"

"A believer, someone who's close to her family, who likes sports, and someone who is honest." He kept his gaze locked on her while he spoke, his voice growing lower by the end of his list.

Her chest rose and fell as he placed his hand on her cheek. She twisted her hips to face him completely, and he leaned forward, his gaze resting on her lips.

Her heart hammered in her chest. Could she really kiss a guy she'd just met yesterday? Before she could decide, Lucas broke the little space between them, gently brushing his lips against hers.

Oh, sweet heaven. Her knees buckled as his cologne enveloped her in a cocoon of nutmeg and sandalwood. Pushing her worries aside, she loosely wrapped her arms around his neck and tipped her chin up, fully giving in to the sweet, delicious kiss.

It was the type of first kiss she never wanted to end. And in that moment, her mind was made up. She couldn't imagine going home, wondering what could have been. She had to break her own rules. With every fiber of her being, she wanted to see if things could work between her and Lucas.

ONE MONTH LATER, ANNIE POINTED OUT OF her car window at a modern red brick building with a large, well-manicured lawn. "And that's where I went to high school."

Lucas rolled down the passenger window and adjusted the baseball cap higher on his forehead. "That place is huge. It's not what I was expecting for a small town."

"I know. It's been remodeled since I graduated. The second story was just added in the last few years. I also heard they put in a coffee shop."

Lucas turned away from the window, raising an eyebrow. "A coffee shop? Do high school kids really need coffee?"

"Apparently." Laughing, she leaned sideways, resting her elbow on the console. Most days, she loved having the console—it had been one of her must-haves when she'd bought the RAV4—but today it was just a nuisance, creating a physical barrier between her and Lucas. They'd seen each other once early in July, but they'd spent most of the month apart and with almost 800 miles between them, the last thing she wanted was distance, even if it was only inches. "Do you want to check out my college next? It's not too far from here and we can walk around campus."

He nodded. "Let's do it."

She drove the short distance to the University of Kansas, speeding into the driveway of the student center and resisting the urge to run around the vehicle to be near him. When she'd picked him up from the airport, they'd hugged and kissed, but even then she'd held back. No one at the airport would want to see a couple passionately kissing.

But now ... She glanced around the almost empty campus as Lucas came up behind her, wrapping his arms around her waist. She leaned into him, resting the back of her head on his shoulder. He put his lips next to her ear. "It's crazy how much I missed you."

Turning around, she yanked off his hat, tossing it on the ground next to them. She ran her fingers through his hair, her chest aching from the weeks they'd spent apart. So much time they could've spent kissing and cuddling. They'd spent hours on Skype and on the phone, but it never felt like enough.

Finally, she pulled back, licking her lips.

Lucas smiled, his blue eyes igniting a flame deep within her core. "You look so relieved."

Annie laughed. For a guy, he could read her pretty well. "I am. I felt a little antsy in the car."

"So what you're saying is that you needed to kiss me?"

"Something like that."

"Feel free to do it anytime you want." Lucas' smile faded slightly. "Except in front of your parents. I'm already nervous enough."

"Why are you nervous? You're the one who wanted to meet them."

Lucas grabbed his hat off the ground, repositioning it on his head. "I want to make a good impression."

"You will." She placed a quick kiss on his lips, reassuring him that her parents would like him. But she couldn't be certain. As the only daughter in her family, her parents had high expectations for her boyfriends. They'd never discouraged her from dating anyone, but they'd also never encouraged her to continue dating anyone either.

So when Lucas had brought up the idea of flying to her hometown to meet her parents, she'd been a little hesitant. Especially because she wasn't sure they were in it for the long haul. She was cautiously optimistic, but it was still too soon to know.

Lucas let go of one of her hands, stepping forward and gently tugging her with him. "Show me everything. I want to see where you ran cross-country, where you lived in your dorm, where you took some of your classes …"

Annie chuckled. How sweet that he was so interested in her past. "I get the picture. I'll show you my freshman dorm first."

"Great." Walking with a bounce in his step, he swung their arms back and forth. "I've been meaning to tell you, my niece really wants to meet you."

"Is this the four-year-old niece you've talked about before?"

"Yeah. I hung out with her last weekend. My dad and I took her to a baseball game."

"Did she like it?"

"She wasn't into the game that much, but she loved the cotton candy I bought her. She had blue all over her face by the time I took her home." Smiling, he ran a hand over his beard. "I don't think my sister was too happy."

Annie shook her head. "Probably not. But that's

what uncles are for, right? You wouldn't be a good uncle if you didn't spoil her."

"You should tell my sister that."

"I can't wait to be an aunt. My oldest brother just got married a couple of months ago, and I know they plan on trying to get pregnant right away."

"Does your brother live nearby?"

"No, both of my brothers moved away after they graduated from college. One lives in Chicago and one lives in Arizona. I wish they lived closer, but we always find excuses to get together."

"I have two sisters, too. One older and one younger."

"This might sound weird, but I like that you come from a family of sisters."

Lucas furrowed his eyebrows, a look of amusement crossing his face. "And why is that?"

"Guys who grow up with sisters are different than guys who grow up with brothers." She glanced up at the clear blue sky, trying to come up with a more specific answer. "They're more sensitive to what a girl needs."

"Ah. Does the same work for girls who grow up with brothers?"

Grinning, she met his gaze. "Of course."

"I'm glad you have two brothers, then." He pulled her closer, wrapping his arm around her waist as they walked up to a tall building with paint chipping off the windowsills. "You know, you have a lot of theories."

"That's because I've dated a lot of people."

"Have your parents met most of them?"

"A good handful of them, yes." She kissed his cheek, sensing his nerves rising again. "Stop worrying. Just enjoy the tour and we'll meet up with my parents for dinner. Okay?"

"You're right." With his arm still around her waist, he gently squeezed her hip. "Is this your old dorm?"

Nodding, she told him about the time when Brooke drove her back to her dorm and got so distracted talking that she turned onto the nearby one-way and had several cars honking at them.

Annie laughed at the humorous memory—she'd experienced several near-death encounters as Brooke's passenger—but on the inside, she was trying to diminish her own worries. Would her parents actually like Lucas? Their approval meant the world to her. Just once she'd love to hear them tell her that they liked a guy, that they could see a future. But she couldn't get her hopes up just yet.

She would know soon enough.

"HOW DO YOU THINK IT WENT?"

"Hold on." Annie readjusted the laptop on her work desk, trying to remove the glare so she could see Lucas in the Skype window.

Once the glare was gone, Lucas came into view, sitting on his bed. He wore athletic pants, a tight pine green shirt that accented his chest muscles, and his favorite baseball cap. Beneath the bill of his hat, his eyebrows creased together in impatience. "Do you think they liked me?"

She picked up her cell. Should she tell Lucas what her mom had said?

"Just tell me the truth."

"Just a sec. Let me pull up the last text my mom sent." She scrolled through her text messages. She probably didn't need to find the text, she'd practically memorized it by now, but she didn't want to mess it up in any way. "This is what my mom said: *I've been praying for a long time for you to meet a godly man. We really like Lucas and look forward to seeing what will happen in the future."*

She glanced up at the computer screen as he let out a whoop, pumping his fist into the air.

Laughing, Annie leaned back in her desk chair and crossed her legs. "You made a really good impression."

"I loved them too. They were so welcoming and nice."

Her heart hitched at the word *love*. After spending the weekend together, showing him her hometown, grilling out with her dad and going to a corn festival with her mom, she hadn't wanted Lucas to leave Kansas. By the time he'd boarded the plane, she knew she was in love with him. And the way he'd looked at her when he said good-bye, she could've sworn she'd seen it in his eyes too. He'd even opened his mouth and shut it as if he'd wanted to say something more, but in the end, he'd left her with a sweet kiss instead.

Now, she had to wonder. What if she was wrong? What if she'd just imagined it, hoping to see something? She didn't know when she'd see him next, and she needed to hear him say it, if only to reaffirm her own feelings.

Moisture built in her eyes and she blinked it

away, grabbing a pen on her desk. She twirled it with her fingers, the movement distracting her from the unanswered questions.

Lucas took off his hat as his eyebrows pinched together. "Why are you upset? Isn't it a good thing your parents like me?"

Annie stopped twirling the pen and clicked the cap open, then shut. "It's not that." *Click, click, click.* She tossed the pen back on her desk. "I don't want to talk about it right now."

Lucas pursed his lips. "Okay." He typed into his computer, excitement sparkling in his pale blue eyes as he glanced at a different part of his computer screen.

"What are you doing?"

"I read about this online sketch pad where you can draw things. I thought it could be a fun way for us to communicate when we're apart."

Smiling, she blinked away the last of her potential tears. Lucas was good at knowing when to press an issue and when to leave it alone. "Will you draw something for me?"

"I already did. I'm pulling it up now." He typed into the computer again.

"Maybe this will make you feel better."

A notepad appeared next to her Skype window with *I love you* scrolled across the middle in big, bold letters.

Her hand flew to her chest and covered her racing heart.

Fresh tears emerged and before she could respond, Lucas spoke. "I'm sorry I didn't say it last weekend. I guess I was waiting for the perfect moment." He bent forward, resting his elbows on his knees. "But I was just talking to a buddy of mine, and he told me to say it if that's how I really feel."

Annie's chest rose and fell as she tried to hold back her emotions to speak clearly. "I love you too."

A grin spread across his face. "I was hoping you would say that."

"I wish I could hug you. I'm glad you told me, but now I miss you more than I did before."

"Let's plan something. I think we'd both feel a lot better if we had a date to look forward to."

"I agree." She glanced at the calendar hanging from her office bulletin board. The next few weekends were filled with a youth pastors' conference, a trip to see her oldest brother, and a half marathon. Maybe she could call her brother and reschedule.

"What do you think about visiting my family in Texas for Thanksgiving?"

"That's almost two months away."

Lucas frowned. "I know it's the longest we've ever spent apart, but I'd like for you to meet my family."

Annie sat up straight, rubbing her sweaty palms against her jeans as she rationalized his offer. She'd been hesitant to let him meet her family and it had turned out great. But meeting his family made her stomach coil with nerves. Their relationship was moving so quickly.

Then again, what was she so afraid of? Except for the distance, everything felt easy with him, like riding one of those roller coasters that shoots you into movement, propelling you forward with seemingly little effort. Just because she'd had complicated relationships in the past didn't mean her relationship with Lucas had to be the same way. And above all, she loved him. Meeting his family was an important step to show him how much she cared.

"So, what do you say?" he asked.

"I'll look for flights tonight."

"Great." Leaning back against a pile of pillows, Lucas put his hands behind his head. "For a second, I thought you would say no. Which is good, because I have something else I want to run past you."

"What is it?"

"I hate the long distance, and I know you do too. I would never ask you to consider leaving a church you love, so I was thinking …" He leaned forward, running a hand over his beard. "Maybe I'll start applying for jobs in Kansas."

Her jaw dropped open. "Are you serious?"

"Yeah. Would that be okay with you?"

A thousand thoughts raced through her mind, sending her thudding heart into overdrive. Talk about fast. They'd only known each other for four months.

But she'd never met anyone like Lucas. He had a strong faith. He fit into her family. He seemed to understand her well, quickly picking up on her non-verbal cues, and he enjoyed deep conversations. *Check, check, check.* So far, he was everything she'd been looking for.

If she was being honest with herself, she had to admit that Lucas could be the one. The thought scared and excited her at the same time.

She smiled at Lucas, a peaceful contentment traveling through her. "Yes, I'd love it if you lived here."

She must be crazy. And yet, she was so, so in love with him.

LISTENING TO PASTOR DOUG, Annie scribbled a To-Do list for the youth group's next fundraiser. Beneath the conference table, she tapped her Converse against the carpet. She'd forgotten her phone at home this morning.

Normally, it wouldn't be a big deal—although she enjoyed snapchatting and texting Lucas throughout her day—but last night, Lucas had been unusually quiet. She'd asked him if anything was wrong and he'd told her that he really missed her and it had been a hard week at work. As the number of unanswered applications rose for engineering companies in Kansas, the more restless he seemed with his job in Texas. Hopefully, he would get an interview soon.

At least she'd see him in a couple of weeks. She'd taken the whole week of Thanksgiving off.

Spending more time together was just what they needed.

Pushing her worries aside, she glanced up at Pastor Doug, adding the remaining items to their To-Do list.

Three hours later, Annie dashed inside her apartment and rushed to the kitchen counter, grabbing her phone. How many missed texts or snapchats did she have from Lucas? She swiped her thumb across the screen, her heart stopping.

No new texts. No snapchats. No missed phone calls.

Her eyebrows furrowed together. How could this be? Her blood boiled. He hadn't contacted her *all* day. How dare he … She stopped her thoughts before they could go any further. She hadn't contacted him either, so she couldn't make a big deal out of it. And he probably had a good reason just like she did.

Taking a deep breath, she walked into the living room and sat down on the couch. She pulled her legs up, resting her elbows on her crisscrossed legs. She ached to hear Lucas' voice, needing his calming reassurance that everything was okay.

Clutching her phone to her ear, she waited for

him to pick up.

"Hi Annie."

"Hey." She paused for a moment, waiting for him to ask why she hadn't texted him. But the line remained silent. "So … did you have a hard day at work?"

"Yeah. You could say that." His voice sounded distant and gravelly.

Annie leaned back against the couch. Her stomach churned. Something was definitely wrong. He purposely hadn't contacted her or else he would've given her an explanation already. "Are you okay?"

He expelled a heavy breath into the receiver. "I can't do this anymore."

"You mean your job?" Part of her felt bad that he was having such a hard time at work, but maybe this was a good thing. Maybe he'd just move to Kansas now. Her spirits lifted a little.

"I'm not talking about my job. I'm talking about us."

Her body stiffened. *Us?* He couldn't be serious. Sure, the distance was hard, but nothing they couldn't handle.

Her heart pounded in her chest, thudding so hard it pulsated in her ears. He'd really said *us*. He wanted to break up.

The walls felt like they were caving in on her, making it difficult to breathe. She untangled her legs and slid off the couch, dropping to the floor. So many questions ran through her mind, they became a jumbled mess. She could barely keep her thoughts straight as they tumbled out of her mouth. "This seems really sudden. Where is this coming from? I mean, how long have you known you wanted to do this?"

"I'm sorry. I'm a jerk."

"I can't believe all the things you've been saying to me. I already bought my plane ticket to visit your family."

"I'm so sorry."

She picked at the strands in her shag rug, tugging at the soft yarn. Small pieces unraveled from the rug, landing in her palm. "Is there anything else you want to say to explain this?"

"I'm not sure what else to say, but I'm sorry."

Annie fumed. Couldn't he say anything else but sorry? She didn't want an apology; she wanted a freaking explanation. That was the least he could do after completely blindsiding her.

The clock on the wall gave a tick, tick, tick,

making each second more noticeable than the first until it became painstakingly obvious that Lucas had nothing better to say.

Her stomach twisted in knots. She pulled the phone away from her ear and clicked the *off* button. The last remnants of shock filtered through her system, replaced by the harsh reality. The transition was so quick it felt like stepping outside on a bitter winter day.

Lucas had just broken up with her.

Annie lowered her whole body onto the rug, lying face up. Her body felt drained of energy, like she'd just completed a long run. Tears welled up in her eyes, spilling down her cheeks. Had she been crazy to think that Lucas was the one?

She had to talk to someone. She needed support.

Still clutching her phone, she scrolled through her contacts to find Brooke's name. Her best friend answered on the third ring. "Hey girl, what's up?"

Annie's chin quivered. "Lucas just broke up with me."

"What?" Brooke's voice raised an octave higher.

"I know." She could just imagine her friend's face, her big brown eyes growing wide.

"What happened?"

"We were talking on the phone, I asked him what was wrong, and he said he couldn't do it anymore." Saying it out loud felt like sticking a dagger deeper into her chest. Tears streamed down her face.

"Did he tell you why?"

"No, that's the worst part." Annie took a deep breath, trying to speak clearly. "He just kept saying sorry over and over again."

"This is nuts. He should've told you why. That's just the decent thing to do."

Annie shook her head. "None of it makes sense, Brooke."

"I don't get it. I just hung out with him last weekend, and he told me how much he loved you. Why would he say that if he was planning on breaking it off?"

A lump formed in her throat. "I feel like such an idiot. How could I be so stupid?"

"Oh, honey. Don't say that. You're not stupid. You were in love with him."

"There must have been signs. I obviously missed them."

"I can't think of any. I honestly thought he was the guy you would marry." As soon as Brooke stopped talking, muffled noises came across the line, followed by a thud.

Annie scrunched her nose. "Where are you?"

"I have to go."

"Why, what are you—"

"I'm at Lucas' house. You deserve an explanation."

She sat straight up, a slight smile tugging at her lips. This was so Brooke, going to her ex's house to fight her battles. "Call me when you leave."

"Of course."

Annie tossed her phone on the rug. She could only imagine the look on Lucas' face when he opened the door to see an angry Brooke standing on his doorstep. Surely, he'd be shocked and dumbfounded.

And she didn't feel sorry for him one bit. She hoped Brooke would lay into him, tell him all the things she'd been too nice to say.

Unfortunately, Lucas might not give Brooke any more information than he'd given her. Most likely, she would never know why he'd suddenly broken up with her.

She draped her arms around her legs, lowering her head against her knees. Her hair glided past her shoulders, creating a curtain of darkness. Where had things gone wrong? Lucas had loved her, she was certain of it. He'd wanted to live near her, to start a life together. He'd never given her any signs that he was unhappy with their relationship.

But she should have known somehow. Her gut should've warned her, but it hadn't. How could she trust her own judgment in the future?

And not only that, how would she be able to trust anyone *ever* again? It seemed impossible.

Annie lifted her head, the glow from the sun radiating through her living room window and caressing her face. She tilted her head back slightly and closed her eyes, soaking in the warmth like a comforting bath.

She had to stop thinking so negatively. Even in the midst of her misery, she could not give in. Impossible was not in her vocabulary. One day she would meet a man who would mend her broken heart.

And maybe he'd be her forever love.

But right now, forever felt like a long time away.

WHERE ARE THEY NOW?

ANNIE AND LUCAS HAVEN'T SPOKEN since their breakup over the phone. Despite Brooke's attempts to get answers, Annie still has no idea why Lucas decided to call it off. Lucas is still living in Texas, working as an engineer. He's dated since Annie but hasn't found the right woman to settle down with.

Annie spends most of her time involved in a variety of church activities. She enjoys running and loves spending time with friends and family, especially now that she's an aunt. She hasn't found the person she wants to spend her life with, but she is optimistic and patient for what the Lord has in store.

Fighting for Us

MEGHAN BALES LEANED BACK in her desk chair and closed her eyes, massaging her throbbing temples. Beneath her desk, she kicked her heels aside and wiggled her cramped toes. Hopefully, her desk created enough of a shadow to cover her shoeless feet. It wasn't professional to take her shoes off at work, but her feet needed room to breathe.

In fact, she needed a few breaths of fresh air, too. When her divorce was finalized months ago, she'd expected to feel relieved, but lately it felt more like drowning. If only she could figure out why. She didn't want to remarry Jeff. She didn't love him anymore, and yet, she couldn't shake the heavy weight pressing against her chest.

Two loud raps knocked on her office door.

Straightening, her eyes flew open as Tom O'Brien strode into the room. He stopped in front of her desk, a glint of humor sparkling in his eyes and a smirk spreading across his clean-shaven face. "Did I catch you at a bad time?"

Meghan shook her head, loose waves falling across her shoulders. "I was just …" She let the sentence trail off, no reasonable excuse coming to mind.

"Taking a morning nap?"

"Taking a break."

His eyes traveled below her desk before meeting her gaze again. "That explains the bare feet."

Heat flamed beneath her cheeks. Of course, he'd notice. Without looking, she slid her feet across the carpet, searching for her shoes.

Tom chuckled and bent down, picking them up. The movement caused his shirt to tighten around his biceps. Her lips parted. When did Tom lose weight and get in shape? She'd worked with him for the last two years, and she'd never noticed.

Then again, she hadn't noticed much of anything lately. Now she looked at Tom as if seeing him in the light for the first time—his dark hair gelled in a conservative cut, his broad shoulders fitting snugly beneath his shirt, and a sun-kissed tan highlighting his bright blue eyes.

Her stomach flip-flopped. Tom was really good-looking.

He cleared his throat, her heels hanging from the tip of his pointer finger.

"Oh, thanks." She grabbed her shoes and slipped them back on her feet.

"I just closed the deal with Sam Leman and Dodge." He set a thick stack of paperwork on her desk. "They want to use our new program at their dealership."

"That's great. You're killing it out there."

A pale pink color crept into his cheeks, giving him a shy, boyish look. "To be honest with you, being a salesman isn't really my thing, but it pays the bills."

"If only you would buy some new Harley shirts with that money." Smiling, she kept her tone light. Everyone at the office knew that Tom kept a bag of undershirts—most of them with Harley logos—behind the desk in his office.

"Hey, there's nothing wrong with my shirts." He crossed his arms, but his lips curled into a grin.

She rolled her eyes. "They're all wrinkled from being smashed into that plastic bag."

"By the time I get home, I have other things to do besides iron my clothes. I have to make dinner for Austin, and then help him with his homework."

"Oh sure, use your son as an excuse." She said it jokingly, but deep down, she understood how hard it was to be a single parent. On the nights she had Hannah, she would leave work, pick her up from preschool, cook dinner, and spend as much quality time with her daughter as possible. No doubt the divorce had hurt Hannah, and Meghan wanted to make sure her little girl still felt loved. Thankfully, Jeff was a good dad and shared joint custody so they could both raise their daughter.

Quick footsteps padded softly down the hallway before their coworker appeared in the doorway. Lily rushed inside Meghan's office, her shiny black hair gliding across her tiny frame. At four-foot nothing, the top of her head made it just above Tom's hip as she stopped beside him, shooting Meghan a curious look. "Did you see how short Veronica's skirt is today? What is she trying to prove?"

Tom uncrossed his arms and knocked on Meghan's desk. "That's my cue to leave." Turning around, he walked out of her office, his dress pants showcasing his trim waist. Meghan wanted to smack her forehead. Seriously, how had she missed Tom's transformation? She'd been too busy replaying shoulda, coulda, woulda in her head, wishing for a reset button on life.

Lily stared at her. "Did I miss something? I'm getting a vibe between you and Tom." She spoke so quickly in her Vietnamese accent, that Meghan barely registered what her coworker had asked.

"Not a thing," she managed.

Lily tapped her foot against the carpet, obviously not buying the answer. But Meghan wouldn't budge. Maybe if she changed the subject, Lily would stop probing. "Do you want to get lunch later? Maybe we could get Pad Thai from Erawan?"

Lily sighed. "Sure, see you later."

As soon as her coworker left, Meghan wondered if she'd made a mistake. Telling Lily how she felt about Tom could be a good idea. Lily had a sisterly, love-hate relationship with Tom. She might have the inside scoop on his dating life.

Too impatient to wait for lunch, Meghan leaned forward, resting her forearms above her cluttered desk and pulled up her email. As she typed a message to Lily, butterflies waltzed across her stomach. She hadn't felt this excited in a long time. *I think I like Tom. Would you talk to him for me? Don't tell him I like him, but maybe hint at it?* Her fingers stopped above the keyboard. What else should she write? *And see if he's interested in me.*

Heart racing, she quickly hit the send button before she could chicken out and delete the email.

Lily immediately wrote back. *You don't have to ask me twice. I'm the queen of matchmaking.*

Meghan's shoulders loosened. *Thank you. I really appreciate it. You have no idea how much this means to me.* Rereading the email thread, she felt a little childish, but if anyone could get answers out of Tom, it would be Lily. Plus, if he didn't want to go out with her, at least she wouldn't get turned down face-to-face.

And yet, what if Tom did like her? A sliver of hope spiraled its way into the crevices of her broken heart, alleviating some of the pressure clinging to her chest.

CLUTCHING A BOUQUET OF FLOWERS, Tom O'Brien walked up to a ranch style house. He still wasn't sure why Meghan had asked him to pick her up at her grandparents' home. Did she live with her grandparents or was she afraid of letting him know where she lived? It's not like he was a stalker, but maybe her divorce had made her overly cautious.

Either way, he still couldn't believe he was going on a date with Meghan, especially since Lily was the one who had started all this. A smile tugged at his lips, his coworker's words coming back all too quickly. *You need to stop taking out floozies and find a nice girl. Like Meghan Bales.*

At first, he'd hesitated. Lily had set him up numerous times—each time with a woman worse than the first, only to find that she'd purposely set him up with women he wouldn't like, thinking it would be funny. When the last woman showed up at Rookies Bar, looking so pale that she glowed in the dark, he'd made a vow never to listen to Lily again, at least not on dating matters.

But when she told him Meghan had a thing for him, he figured this time was different. He actually knew Meghan.

He stepped onto the porch and rang the doorbell. Musical chimes rang through the house, loud enough for him to hear outside. As he waited, uncertainty vibrated through his core. Even though Meghan was interested in him, he still had doubts. They were very different people. For starters,

Meghan looked several years younger than him. Surely she was in her early twenties while he was in his mid-thirties. Sometimes, she gave off the impression that she was a little snooty, and she was much quieter than him.

But he was willing to give tonight a chance. They got along well at work, so if anything, they'd have an enjoyable night, and go back to being coworkers tomorrow.

The door opened and a woman wearing an apron stood in the foyer. Her steel-blue eyes assessed him from head to toe before her gaze fell on the bouquet. She put a hand over her heart, her expression softening. "Oh my. You brought Meghan flowers?"

"Yeah. I mean, yes."

"That's so sweet."

He twisted the bouquet in his hands.

A short, slender man with white hair and glasses stepped into the foyer, carrying a newspaper under his armpit. He shook his head. "Evelyn, you're embarrassing the boy. The least you could do is let him into the house."

She waved her hand dismissively. "Oh, Charlie. Hush."

Tom smiled. He definitely wasn't a boy anymore, but if Meghan's grandpa thought he looked young enough to be a boy, he couldn't help liking the guy. So he walked inside, offered his hand and introduced himself, making small talk while he waited for Meghan.

A few minutes later, the stairs creaked and he turned his head, swallowing hard. Meghan was naturally beautiful, but he hadn't seen her wear much makeup to work in a long time, not since her divorce. It wasn't just the makeup, though, her eyes sparkled with vibrancy, and it wasn't until now that he realized how much he'd missed the old Meghan.

When she stopped in front of him, he sucked in a breath and handed her the flowers. "You look great."

"Thank you." She smiled like a giddy schoolgirl and brought the flowers to her nose. "No one's ever given me flowers before. They smell wonderful." She looked at her grandma. "Would you mind putting them in a vase for me?"

"Of course." Evelyn squeezed Meghan's arm and put a hand behind Tom's back, nudging him toward the door. "Enjoy your dinner. Now, shoo, you don't want to spend your whole night with us old people."

Tom chuckled, leading Meghan to his Taurus. On the way to the restaurant, he switched the radio to 1420 Talk Radio and let the station fill the silence.

Eventually, Meghan turned toward him, her hands clasped firmly between her legs. "You definitely won over my grandma. She couldn't take her eyes off you."

"I can take her out tomorrow night if she wants."

"Very funny." Meghan unclasped her hands and played with a loose thread on her sweater. "But really, it means a lot to me to have my grandparents approve. They are a huge part of my life. They've always been there for me when I needed them." She twirled the loose thread around her finger. "In fact, they've been letting Hannah and I stay with them."

"Wow, that's great."

"Their house is like a sanctuary. I'm going to miss it when we move out."

"Are you moving soon?"

"Yeah, I just found an apartment. I'm in the process of getting it all set up."

"They seem like very genuine people. I really like your grandpa."

Meghan grinned. "He might not like you too much after you take out my grandma tomorrow night."

"Oh man, that's true." Tom chuckled. Meghan had acted nervous at first, but she seemed to be loosening up. Hopefully, that meant he was doing something right. "On second thought, I'll just stick with their granddaughter."

"Grandma will be disappointed." Meeting his gaze, Meghan's smile grew as he pulled into the parking lot at El Rodeo.

He opened the car door for her and led her inside, admiring her from behind. Meghan had that perfect hourglass shape. He hadn't noticed how good-looking she was, assuming they'd never be a good match.

The hostess ushered them to a bright red booth at the back of the restaurant. The wall beside the booth was painted with a man riding a horse, tipping his sombrero at a woman in a big flowery dress. Small, decorative piñatas hung from the ceiling, one directly above their table. A waiter set down a bowl full of chips and a jar of salsa. "Be right back to get your drinks, amigos."

The waiter rushed away and Tom pulled back a

chair, gesturing for Meghan to sit.

"Thank you. You're quite the gentleman."

He shrugged and took a seat across the table. He didn't always do this for his dates, but he knew how much Meghan was hurting from the divorce—the light had gone out of her eyes and her vivacious spirit had disappeared—so tonight, he was going to treat her right. She deserved it.

The waiter came back and took their food and drink orders, then silence settled over the table. Tom picked up a chip and dipped it in salsa. He racked his brain for something to say, but a strong odor permeated the air, making it hard to think straight.

Across the table, Meghan waved a hand in front of her nose. "Does something smell funky to you?"

"Yes, like a park bathroom."

"Trying to be covered up with Pine Sol," she added, giggling. How long had it been since he'd heard that beautiful sound?

The waiter dropped off their margaritas, and Tom leaned back in his chair, crossing a bent leg over his knee. Taking a drink, he glanced at Meghan above the salt-covered rim of his glass. "I've missed your laugh."

She stared at him for a moment, noticeably swallowing. "You have?"

"Yeah. You're so serious sometimes; I like making you laugh."

She took a sip from her straw, a smile spreading across her face. "You're pretty good at it."

"Not lately."

"Well, there are a lot of reasons for that. I wasn't going to say anything, but I might as well tell you." Leaning forward, she crossed her legs and set her elbows on the table. "I'm quitting."

"Really?"

"Yeah, I've been thinking about it for a while now. It's not a good fit for me."

Disappointment settled in his gut. Work wouldn't be the same without her. "Do you have another job lined up?" He picked up a handful of chips, taking a bite of one.

"I just applied to Strieter Lincoln Mercury, and I'm pretty sure I got the job. I plan on working there for a few years, until I can open an at-home day care."

A chip dropped out of his hand. He'd always thought Meghan was the businesswoman type, but her career aspirations showed a maternal side that he hadn't seen in the office. "That's cool. Would you take kids of all ages?"

Meghan nodded. "I love babies, so I'd watch kids from newborn to pre-K. I think it'd be a lot of fun."

He let out a low whistle. "I can't imagine taking care of more than a few kids at a time. At least you're young enough to have the energy for it."

She raised her eyebrows. "How old do you think I am?"

"In your early twenties." His cheeks filled with warmth, and he hoped she wasn't offended.

Meghan smiled. "That's really nice of you, but I'm twenty-eight."

"I'm not trying to be nice, you look like you're in your early twenties." He shifted in his seat, pleased that she took his wrong assumption as a compliment, and even more pleased that they were closer in age than he'd thought. "Austin was all over the place when he was a toddler. I couldn't sit down for a second without him opening cabinets or putting something in his mouth. I was always afraid he would choke."

"How old is he now?"

"Eleven. How old is Hannah?"

"Three." Meghan rubbed the edge of her glass with her thumb. "It's amazing that you've taken care of Austin all by yourself. I'm sure it was hard."

"Well, Austin's mom is still in the picture. She and I dated for about seven years. In the end, we wanted to make it work, but we knew we weren't right for each other." He grabbed a napkin, running it over his hands. "Looking back, I wouldn't have it any other way. Austin's the best thing that's ever happened to me." As hard as it was sometimes, he loved being a dad, taking Austin boating on the river, playing videogames together, driving around and looking at houses.

They'd been doing pretty well on their own, and most of the time, he liked being a single dad. But he couldn't deny that sometimes he missed having a woman's nurturing presence in their lives. Someone he could come home to, who would hug him when he got home from work, someone who had more patience to cook a better meal than spaghetti, someone to lie in bed with at night.

A few feet away, beef and shrimp tacos sizzled on hot plates that the waiter balanced above his hands. "Here you go, amigos." Placing the meals on the table, he glanced at their half-empty margaritas.

"More drinks?"

Tom exchanged a glance with Meghan, who shook her head.

The waiter gave them two thumbs up before turning on his heels and walking to the back room.

Picking up her fork, Meghan's gaze returned to Tom.

"What?"

"I'm really impressed by you." She moved her fork with her hand as she spoke. "I know you're making it sound like no big deal, but being a single dad for eleven years—doing all the housework, taking care of all the bills, raising a son—that's a lot for one person to handle."

He shrugged.

"That would be enough to give me a nervous breakdown."

Tom wiped away the perspiration dripping down his margarita glass. "You're making me sound like some kind of hero."

"I'm serious. Like sitting in the corner of the room, rocking back and forth, putting on lipstick—that kind of nervous breakdown."

He raised an eyebrow. "Where did that come from?"

"I don't know." She broke into a smile, then covered her mouth with her hand, giggling.

Her giggle was contagious, and before he knew it, laughter bubbled in his chest as he imagined the crazy person in the corner that she'd described.

People from nearby tables glanced in their direction, but he didn't care. This date was going way better than he'd imagined. He had a lot in common with Meghan. They were both close to their grandparents, they were single parents, and they had a similar sense of humor. Maybe this relationship could work, after all.

But even though he'd been wrong about their differences, there was still one major concern he needed to address.

At the end of the night, he walked Meghan to the doorstep of her grandparents' house. They left the porch light on, and it illuminated the dark irises of her eyes as she looked up at him. "Thank you for a wonderful night."

"It was my pleasure." Tom squeezed the back of his neck, trying to think of the best way to bring up his concern. "Can I ask you a question?"

She bit her lip. "What is it?"

"Are you ready to be in a relationship?"

She dug the heel of her boot into the porch, and he could sense her considering the weight of his question. "Before tonight, I wasn't sure. But after going out with you, I'd like to see what could happen between us." Pausing, she reached for his hand and squeezed it. "I like us."

The full impact of her words sent his heart thudding into overdrive. He had no more qualms, no more questions about whether they'd be a good couple. He had no doubt they would be.

He stepped closer to her and set his hands on her waist, dipping his head so their faces were inches apart.

She held his steady gaze, her lips parting slightly.

"Can I kiss you?" His voice came out hoarse, like it was trapped in his throat.

She nodded after a moment and smiled. "Yes."

He broke the distance between them, his lips meetings hers. He kissed her gently, holding back, not wanting to press too far. She ran her fingers through his hair, her lips becoming soft. Tingles of electricity shot through his body, pooling warmth into his core.

Using all the self-control he had, he pulled back, keeping his face close to hers. "Man, I'll have to thank Lily for the one good thing she did for me."

Meghan laughed. "I know, right? She is a good matchmaker after all."

Three years later …

"BYE, SEE YOU TOMORROW." Meghan forced a smile and waved good-bye to the last parent picking up a child from her at-home day care. As the parent's van backed out of the driveway, she shut the door, and the tension in her shoulders loosened slightly. Now that all the kids were gone, she didn't have to pretend to be the happy day care provider anymore.

She trudged into the kitchen and sank into a chair, glancing at her watch. Tom should already be home, but of course he wasn't. He hadn't been home on time in the last few months.

Meghan twisted the wedding ring on her finger. Where had her relationship with Tom gone wrong? After their first dinner at El Rodeo, they'd dated for a year, and she'd fallen hopelessly in love with him. He was a great guy—respectful, funny, hardworking, and best of all, a good father. He treated

Hannah like his own daughter. And after they got married and had Aidan, she saw firsthand how patient he was raising a little one.

"Mom." Hannah rushed into the kitchen with Aidan trailing behind her. "I think he pooped. His diaper really stinks."

Meghan lifted her son's shirt and pulled back his diaper, taking a whiff. "You're right. Will you get a diaper for me?"

"Okeydokey. Come on Aidan, follow me."

Meghan glanced at her watch again. Her chest tightened. Questions probed her heart, stinging like needles. Didn't Tom want to come home and see her? Didn't he miss spending time with her and the kids?

Maybe she should have taken more time to heal from her last relationship before marrying him. Then again, she never would've dated Tom because she left Dealer Marketing Services days after their dinner at El Rodeo.

Marrying Tom and starting a day care hadn't turned out like she'd hoped. Being home all day provided way too much time to think. Little arguments she had with Tom festered inside of her until he got home, and the little arguments turned into full-blown fights, especially about how to raise their stepchildren.

She buried her head in her hands. Did he even love her anymore? If not, what was she supposed to do?

One year later …

MEGHAN RESTED HER BACK AGAINST the headboard of her bed and slid her arm out of the thick comforter, reaching for the remote. She aimlessly flipped from channel to channel, but nothing caught her attention. Finally, she hit the power button, silence filling her apartment. How many times had she wished for a morning like this? A quiet, lazy morning just by herself without rushing Austin and Hannah off to school, or dashing through the house preparing for the day care kids, or arguing with Tom before he left for work?

A tear slipped down her cheek. Being alone in this new apartment was anything but peaceful. Not when a turmoil of emotions squeezed her insides so tightly she could barely breathe. A year ago, she'd asked for a separation. They'd lived together through most of it, until a few days ago when Tom had the official separation papers served to her. Now, she was second-guessing everything.

Sniffling, more tears streamed down her face. She sank down into the mattress, burying her head under the comforter as sobs rocked her body. Unlike her first divorce, this didn't feel right. Without Tom, a part of her was missing. She needed him. Like a traveler walking through the desert, he was her water source.

She turned onto her stomach and screamed into the pillow. She let everything out—all the hurt, the anger, the bitterness. She continued screaming until her voice grew hoarse and her throat felt raw.

Flipping over to her side, she stared at the almost empty nightstand, her gaze resting on her cell phone. She yearned to call Tom and tell him that she didn't want a divorce. But she couldn't say that, not when she'd been the one to ask for a separation in the first place.

And yet, she desperately wanted to hear his voice. She reached for her phone, scrolling through her contacts, and clicked on his name.

Seconds later, Tom's voice came out sharp,

slicing through her heart. "What?"

She swallowed hard, fighting the urge to hang up, to give up on their relationship for good. "I wanted to hear your voice."

"Okay."

"I know you're mad."

Tom sighed into the receiver, and she could just imagine him running a hand through his hair. "Look, we're a week away from signing the divorce papers. I just want to get this over with."

Her lips trembled. Did he really mean that or was it his anger speaking? She sat up against the headboard, knowing she had to make this right. She couldn't lose him. "Would you meet me for lunch?"

He didn't answer.

"Please." This time, she wasn't asking.

"Okay."

Meghan's eyes widened and a touch of a smile graced her lips. It was time to get her husband back.

She took a quick shower, put on a new outfit, did her hair and makeup, and rushed to the café where they'd planned to meet.

Tom sat at a table in the middle of the restaurant dressed in jeans and the new Harley T-shirt she'd bought him for his birthday. His brown hair was evenly gelled and his face clean-shaven. Her stomach catapulted upside down. He wanted to look nice for her. Did that mean she had a chance?

Sliding into the chair across from him, her mouth went dry. "Thank you for coming."

"What's going on?" Tom leaned forward, resting his forearms on the table. His hard, downcast gaze turned her heart to stone, and a lump formed in her throat.

He had every right to be mad at her; she was the one who'd asked for the separation, but his brash tone felt like a slap on her face. Couldn't he at least treat her like he still cared?

She tapped her shoe against the floor. This was it. She had to lay it all out there. She crossed her legs, trying to contain the adrenaline pumping through her. "I'm so sorry, for everything. I love you and I miss you. I know we have a long way to go to make things right between us, but I'm willing to try."

Tom gripped his coffee mug on the table. "I don't know what to say. I thought you wanted a divorce." Forming a fist, he lightly hit the table. "I mean, we're going to court next week, and now you've changed your mind?"

"Better late than never, right?" It sounded meek, even to her ears, but she had to convince him it wasn't too late.

He grunted. "No. It's not better. I'm trying to move on, to look forward, not back."

She shook her head, wishing she could shake away his words. He didn't understand. It wasn't too late. She reached across the table and took his hands, cupping them in her own. "Do you still love me?"

Meghan's heart pulsed in her ears as she waited for an answer. If he didn't love her anymore, she had no idea what she'd do. She couldn't force him to have feelings for her.

His Adam's apple bobbed up and down. "Yes. I still love you."

She expelled a relieved breath. "Let's go to counseling, then. I don't want to give up on us." She resisted the urge to jump out of her seat and kiss him, to show him how serious she was, but he still looked hesitant.

"Let me think about it."

Leaning back in her chair, she slid her hands away from his, and bit the inside of her cheek to keep from screaming. *No, you don't need more time. Fight for me, fight for us, starting now.* But she couldn't. He needed to make up his mind, and she had to wait.

Did she have a chance? She glanced at Tom, hoping for some glimmer of hope, but he was staring out the window, a distant gaze in his eyes.

5 Years later …

TOM STEPPED ONTO THE FLORIDA BEACH with bare feet. Soft particles of sand squeezed between his toes. In the distance, the sun peeked above the horizon, washing the sky with pink, yellow, and red watercolors. The tide was just coming in, splashing against the shore. The view was breathtaking.

But as he glanced at Meghan beside him, he couldn't look away. She wore a white, lacey, knee-length dress that accented her hourglass figure. Her reddish-blond hair hung in loose waves below her shoulders and her hazel eyes searched deep inside of him. He reached for her hand, lacing their fingers together as they strolled toward the ocean.

Meghan looked down at her feet. "You know what's kinda funny?"

"What?"

"When I first started falling for you, I was shoe-less then too."

Tom chuckled. "How could I forget? You were taking that much-needed nap … Oh, I mean *break*, right?"

She let out a playful growl. "I'll never live that down. I swear I wasn't asleep."

"Uh-huh, sure."

"Are you guys coming?" Aidan's voice traveled above the tide, and Tom turned his attention to Hannah and Aidan. Hannah stood at the tip of the shore, careful not to get water on her dress. Too bad Austin couldn't be here, too, but he was taking classes at the University of Iowa.

The kids had been looking forward to this moment for the last few months, ever since Meghan had suggested they renew their vows. It still felt unreal that five years ago, they had been one week away from getting a divorce. But after Meghan's apology and plea that day at lunch, he knew she was right. They *were* worth fighting for. She had been the missing link all those years when he was a bachelor, and when she moved out of the house during their separation, his life was torn apart like a thread slowly unraveling from a shirt until it was no longer whole.

Of course, they had fought an uphill battle. Working through their issues and opening old wounds wasn't easy. But their marriage counselor had suggested a *Men Are From Mars and Women Are From Venus* class, and it was just what they'd needed. It made him realize his mistakes and helped him learn how to become a better husband. He knew that Meghan deserved nothing less from him.

Hannah dashed up to Meghan and playfully nudged her in the side. "Are we doing this or what?"

Laughing, Meghan ran a hand through Hannah's short dark hair. "We aren't in a hurry tonight. We're going to soak up this moment for all its worth."

Aidan skipped toward them. "I think you should stop right here. It's the perfect spot."

"I think you're right, buddy." Tom stood still, pulling Meghan to his side and kissing her cheek.

Hannah put a hand on her hip. "I thought you weren't supposed to kiss until we say, '*you may now kiss the bride.*'"

"That's true most of the time," Meghan said.

"But we're just saying our vows," Tom added.

When they'd first started planning this trip, they wanted to ask their pastor to officiate and invite several of their friends, but as the weeks went by, they decided to make it simple. In the end, it really came down to what was most important. And after working so hard to repair their marriage, their change of heart was all that mattered. They could speak these vows with more love and confidence than ever before.

Tom wrapped his arms around Meghan's lower back, pulling her close until there was no space left between them. He pressed his lips against hers, kissing her with a renewed fire that ignited in his chest and burned through his entire body.

He would never let the flames go out again.

WHERE ARE THEY NOW?

MEGHAN AND TOM HAVE BEEN MARRIED for almost eleven years. They live in Davenport, Iowa. They enjoy spending time together as a family, hiking, and taking long walks on the beach—preferably in Destin, Florida.

Playing for Keeps

"HERE YOU GO." JENNY KRIESEL handed a steaming hot dog and a container of nachos to the teenage boy across the counter. Taking his cash, she pointed to the side of the concession stand. "Ketchup and mustard are over there."

"Thanks." The boy's voice cracked at the end of the word, and his cheeks burned bright red beneath the bill of his baseball cap. Grabbing his food, he spun around and scurried toward the stands.

Jenny held back a grin. Teenagers could be so endearingly awkward. No doubt she'd have numerous awkward moments teaching and coaching. That is, when she found a job, but right now it looked pretty bleak. It was already July, and school would start in August.

She'd applied for every opening in Wisconsin. After spending so much time in college studying, creating lessons, and writing curriculums, she couldn't wait to get in the classroom and practice everything she'd learned. If she didn't get an interview soon, she'd apply for her substitute license and work on making connections with local school districts. That way she could still live close to her family.

"Heads up!" several voices screamed from the stands.

She glanced at the baseball field as a ball flew down the first baseline, straight toward her. Crouching down, she ducked behind the counter and covered her head with her hands. A loud thump struck the back wall of the concession stand, and then the ball bounced to the floor.

She lowered her arms, expelling a frustrated breath. How many more foul balls would the Eau Express hit today? They needed to get it together.

"Are you all right?" Michael Lauritsen leaned over the counter, his chocolate brown eyes peering down at her beneath long, dark lashes.

"I'm okay. It didn't hit me." Jenny stood and met his gaze, heat warming her cheeks. Just last week, she'd been messaging her friend Brian, asking about Michael. She'd seen him with Brian at several Eau Express games this summer, and she wanted to know more about him.

Michael slipped his hands inside the pockets of his faded khaki shorts, a warm smile spreading across his face. With dark hair, an oval face, long slender nose, and full lips, he looked like a young version of Jerry Seinfeld. "You're not in a good spot today."

"I know. I have a whole bucket of foul balls back here." She reached down and picked up the latest ball, tossing it in the bucket.

"Maybe they're purposely aiming for you, trying to get your attention."

Her stomach dipped in an airy somersault. Was he flirting with her or was she just imagining it? Before she could think about it for too long, she realized he was waiting for her to respond. "They'd better stop, or they'll lose the game."

Footsteps clanged against the metal stands and ended with a thump as Brian hopped off and landed on the concrete. He walked toward the concession stand, looking from Jenny to Michael. His lips drew into a thin line. "Is Jenny refusing you service or did she run out of T-shirts?"

Michael rocked back on his heels, a sheepish grin on his face. "I haven't asked her yet."

"Oh." Brian crossed his arms, his tone sharp and clipped.

Jenny chewed on her thumbnail. What was up with Brian? Usually, he was in a good mood. Unless … Did he like her? They'd been talking a lot this summer, but he'd never asked her out. She unclasped her hair tie, letting loose blond strands fall to her shoulders before she scooped them up in a low ponytail. If he did have feelings for her, he was surely hurt after their conversation about Michael.

Shoot.

Michael leaned over, resting his tan forearms on the counter. "About that shirt."

Grateful for the distraction, she moved toward the back wall, lined with Eau Express apparel. "Are you sure you want one after the way they're playing today?"

Scowling, he held up his hands, palms forward. "What do you think I am, a fair-weather fan?"

"Just checking." She laughed. "Which one do you want?"

"The orange one."

Jenny pulled a T-shirt off the hanger and walked back to the counter, folding it.

"You don't have to do that. I'm going to wear

it." Reaching for the shirt, his hand brushed against hers.

Despite the warm weather, shivers ran up and down her arm. She took a quick breath, trying to stay composed. Michael made it hard as he pulled the new T-shirt down over the one he already wore. Before he could adjust the length, his undershirt lifted, exposing a hard, lean stomach.

Daaang. He was in good shape. She imagined running her hands over his stomach then stopped her thoughts. What was wrong with her? She barely knew him, and she needed to consider what Brian had told her. Michael was moving out of state—not the best time to start a relationship, *if* he was even interested in her.

Tugging the shirt over his belt, Michael caught her lingering gaze and smirked.

She looked away, blushing like she'd been caught doing something wrong. This was probably how the students felt during her student teaching when she'd caught them passing notes.

Brian patted Michael on the back. "Ready to go, man? We're missing the game."

Michael stood rooted in place, keeping his gaze locked on Jenny. "Do you work the entire game?"

"No, I'm done after the seventh inning."

"If you want to watch the rest of it with us, we're sitting behind the third baseline." Without waiting for her to respond, he turned and followed Brian up the stands.

Excitement bubbled in her chest. She would take any opportunity to talk more with Michael. From what she knew so far, he was outgoing and confident, and he seemed like the kind of guy who liked to joke around.

But she couldn't deny the guilt settling in like a dense fog, dimming her excitement. She'd met Brian first, and she'd never given him a chance. If only she'd sensed his feelings sooner, she wouldn't have asked him about Michael. She didn't want to hurt him. Brian was a nice guy.

She'd be spending time with both of them this afternoon. Maybe then she'd have a better idea of her feelings, if she even had a choice. Michael might have asked her to sit with them because he was being nice.

She frowned. Hopefully, that wasn't the case.

The crowd jumped out of their seats, clapping. She turned her attention to the field just as Schmidt rounded third base, running for home. One of the outfielders caught the ball and threw it to their catcher. Schmidt dove for the plate, arms outstretched.

She put two fingers in her mouth and let out a shrill whistle. "Hurry!"

Schmidt's fingers touched the plate seconds before the catcher caught the ball in his mitt.

"Yes!" She jumped up and down, pumping her fist in the air.

A woman and three children walked up to the concession stand and ordered Snickers bars, followed by a silver-haired couple asking for Dip'N Dots. On the field, the Eau Express struck out and the Bucks scored two runs. She tried to stay focused on the customers and the game, but she kept thinking about Michael.

A deep voice came over the loud speaker, introducing the choir from Franklin Elementary School. Soft, high-pitched voices sang, "Take me out to the ball game ..." The crowd stood for the seventh inning stretch, singing along with the choir.

Go time. With sweaty hands, she counted the money in the register, reorganized the apparel, and locked the concession stand. She rolled up the sleeves of her gray work shirt and ran a wet cloth over a grease stain on her khaki shorts. The stain smeared into a large wet blob. *Great, now it looks even more obvious.* Sighing, she tossed the cloth on the counter.

She hadn't felt this nervous in a long time. She'd gone on several dates during college, but none of them had turned into anything serious. Hopefully, Michael wouldn't notice her inexperience.

Well, she couldn't do anything about it now. Ignoring her nerves, she walked past several families and couples leaving the game early. She took the steps up two at a time, heading toward one of the middle rows behind third base.

Michael saw her coming down the stairs, a hint of a smile gracing his lips. "You survived the shift."

"I wasn't sure I would. That one foul ball came pretty close to my head."

She slid into the open seat next to him and slipped a pair of small oval sunglasses over her eyes.

Brian leaned forward in his seat, resting his elbows on his knees. "It's been a rough summer for the team. They lost Thompson to a knee injury, and the new pitcher is only a sophomore. He's not very good."

Michael chuckled. "And yet, we still come to

watch them play."

Brian glanced at Jenny before directing his gaze to the field. He adjusted his ball cap, lowering it over his forehead.

A lump formed in her throat. She had the sinking feeling that he'd been coming to the games to see her. She opened her mouth, and then shut it, searching for something to say to either Michael or Brian. "What are you guys doing for the Fourth of July?"

Brian perked up a little, glancing her way. "Nothing yet. You?"

"I don't have any plans either. Usually, my friends and I throw a party. But most of them moved back home after graduation." She chewed on her nails nonchalantly. "Maybe you could have a party at your place, Brian."

"That's a good idea."

Michael put his palm up to stop further conversation, a glint of humor sparkling around the dark irises of his eyes. "Shouldn't you ask your landlord if it's okay?"

"Nah, he's my friend so he'll be fine with it." Brian shrugged. "And if he's not, then I won't ask him to come to baseball games with me anymore."

"Wait a minute." Jenny took off her sunglasses and twisted toward Michael. "You're a landlord?"

"Yeah."

"Aren't you a little young? I mean, when I think of a landlord, I usually imagine an older guy."

"I joined AARP last year, but I'm their youngest member."

"Very funny." Rolling her eyes, she leaned back in her seat and crossed her legs. Michael was full of surprises. She wished she could get to know him better before he moved, whenever that was. Hopefully, there was time. "So … is this party happening or what?"

Brian nodded. "Heck yes."

"Awesome." She rubbed her palms together in excitement, giving Michael a sideways glance. "Are you going?"

"I'll think about it." Michael wore a serious expression as he spoke, pausing for a moment before his mouth curled up on one side in a sexy smirk.

Jenny shook her head. He was clearly trying to play hard to get. *I'll think about it* had to be code for yes. It just had to.

MICHAEL LAURITSEN PARKED HIS TRUCK in front of Capper's Restaurant. The fading sun peeked behind the two-story brick building, casting a dimming glow on Lake Wissota just beyond. It was a great place for a first date.

Jenny peered out the passenger window. Her ponytail glided over her slender shoulder, and he had the sudden urge to toss it over her back. But he wouldn't. Tonight was all about showing her that he could be a gentleman to make up for the Fourth of July party. Things got a little too out of hand that day—first with several rounds of tippy cup, then out to the bars, where they'd had their first kiss.

The memory of that kiss still brought warmth pooling low into his stomach. "Life is a Highway" had started playing over the bar's loudspeakers, and he'd pulled Jenny out onto the crowded dance floor. Blue and yellow strobe lights illuminated her face as she let out a giggle and they moved to the fast beat of the song. They sang along, their voices barely audible above the loudspeakers. He drank her in, watching her let loose, her arms swaying in the air.

And suddenly, he couldn't hold back any longer. He put his hand on the small of her back and dipped her, their faces inches apart. She met his gaze for a moment before she looked at his lips. Then his mouth was on hers, and they kissed with a wild starvation. He brought her to a standing position and she put her hands against his chest, the kiss hot and pressing. His heart thudded fast and loud, and he tried to calm down.

He pulled away slowly, prepared to apologize. He hadn't meant to give her more than a peck. But when he looked at Jenny, a wide smile spread across her face. She'd enjoyed that kiss as much as he had.

Now, he turned off the truck and pushed the memory away. If he thought about it for too long, he'd probably end up kissing her again. "Ready?" he asked.

Nodding, Jenny grabbed her clutch and reached for the door handle.

"Wait. I'll get it." He jumped out of his truck and jogged around to the front, opening her door. Holding out his hand, he helped her down—not without noticing how well her palm fit inside his.

He didn't let go of her hand as they made their way toward the restaurant. Inside, the young hostess greeted them with a polite smile. Michael leaned forward, whispering to the hostess, asking for outside seating. The girls at his office said the restaurant had a great view of the lake from the open second story.

"Sure," the hostess said.

Jenny gave him a curious glance. "Telling secrets? Should I be concerned?"

"Nah, I'm not going to propose or anything."

"Oh good." Smiling, she nudged his shoulder with hers. "Cause I'd say no."

Michael chuckled. He liked that Jenny was the type of girl who could hold her own.

The hostess reached for two thick menus, clutching them against her black button down shirt. "Follow me."

He let Jenny walk in front of him up the stairs. It was the gentlemanly thing to do, plus it gave him a chance to check out how snugly her jeans fit around her long, lean legs and how her pink top showcased her athletic, yet feminine build—the perfect body type in his opinion.

"Oh wow." Jenny stopped at the top of the stairs, her gaze traveling across the wooden deck. White lights ran along the pergola roof, highlighting the black linen tablecloths with candle centerpieces. "It's so pretty up here."

"I'm glad you like it."

"Have you been here before?"

"No, I asked some of my coworkers for recommendations, and they suggested this place. I told them I wanted somewhere nice, yet different. I didn't want to take you somewhere you've been before."

"That was sweet of you."

They followed the hostess to a table near the side of the deck, directly overlooking the lake. The dark water sparkled beneath the descending sun. A speedboat drove past, splashing water against the shore beneath.

Great spot. He slipped into a seat across from Jenny, mesmerized by the reflection of candlelight in her sea-blue eyes. He was barely aware of the hostess going through the list of specials, asking for drink orders, and leaving the table.

Jenny met his gaze. "I'm glad you decided to go to the party. I had fun with you."

"I had a good time with you too."

"Just so you know, I don't usually …" A faint hue of red graced her cheeks as she unrolled her silverware, laying it neatly across her lap. "Kiss someone I barely know."

"Me either." Michael smiled. She looked cute

when she was embarrassed.

"I think Brian had a good time too. Did he ever call that girl he was talking to at Cubbies?"

"I doubt it. Brian just likes to flirt." Leaning back in his chair, Michael bent one leg and rested it above his knee.

A pleased expression crossed Jenny's face. "I see."

"What is it?"

"I thought Brian liked me, and I felt bad because I didn't realize it until I asked him about you."

He chuckled. "Well, you weren't wrong about that. He did have a crush on you, but when he saw how well we hit it off, he decided not to ask you out."

"He's not mad at us, is he?"

Michael shook his head, remembering his conversation with Brian. "He's a little disappointed, but he thinks we'd be good together."

"I hope he's right," she said softly.

Smiling, he leaned forward, resting his forearms on the table. "So, you asked about me?"

The faint hue in her cheeks turned bright crimson. She picked up her fork, running her thumb across the smooth handle. "Maybe ..."

"It's a little late to claim innocence now."

"Oh man." She laughed, the gentle sound as soothing as a boat ride on the river.

A short, plump waitress stopped by their table with two glasses of white wine and a metal container full of seasoned bread. She poured olive oil on their small plates then took their food orders. "I'll be back shortly."

Michael picked up his wine, taking a drink. He wanted to ask her what Brian had said, but then thought better of it. She seemed embarrassed, and he didn't want to put her on the spot.

In the silence, classical music played softly from the speakers. Jenny cleared her throat. "Brian mentioned something that I'm curious about."

"What's that?"

"That you're moving."

He grabbed a piece of bread and dipped it in olive oil, contemplating what to say. He hadn't planned on telling her about the move yet. It was still so early in their relationship, and he didn't want to put pressure on them. Or worse, he didn't want her to end things.

He sat up straighter in his chair. Hopefully, she would give him a chance. "It's true. I'm moving to

Iowa to start my own irrigation company."

"Wow, that's a big undertaking."

"Yeah, it is. But my dad has a lot of connections and experience, so he plans on helping me at first."

Jenny reached for her wine, swirling it around in the glass. "How long before you move?"

"Seven months."

"Oh." Her lips drew into a thin line. She set her glass back down on the table without taking a drink.

"I hope you're not mad I didn't tell you sooner. I like you, and I wanted to see if we had potential first. I mean, I already know we have chemistry so …" He let the sentence trail off, wishing he could find the right words.

Her eyes filled with understanding. "I'm not mad. I'd like to spend more time with you, though."

"I agree." He expelled a relieved breath. She wanted to see him again. "I know my move complicates things, but I'd like to see where this relationship can go."

Jenny noticeably swallowed. A slow smile spread across her face. "I want that too."

A weight he didn't even realize was there lifted off his shoulders. He leaned over the table and kissed her softly on the lips. Seven months was a long time to find out if they had potential. And he had a good feeling that they did.

"I GOT THE JOB." Clutching the steering wheel with one hand, Jenny positioned her cell phone between her ear and shoulder. "The principal offered me a job on the spot."

The line went silent for a moment. Her heart raced, waiting for Michael to respond.

"That's awesome."

"Uh-huh."

"When do you start?"

"This week."

"*This* week?"

"Yeah." Jenny tried to keep her tone steady, but her bottom lip trembled. She'd hoped to get the job when she'd interviewed, but now that she had it, reality was sinking in. She'd have to move two hours away to Viroqua, Wisconsin. At the beginning of the summer, moving to a new town would've been exciting. But now, moving away from Michael felt daunting.

"Did you like the school?" he asked.

"Yeah, the principal was really nice, and ..." She had more positive things to say about the school, but her chest was aching, making it difficult to concentrate. She'd spent so much time with Michael since their first date a month ago—boating on the river, whitewater kayaking, canoeing, and attending Country JAM.

They still had six months before Michael moved. But now, months had turned into days. Could they handle a long-distance relationship? No more long runs together, or going to Eau Claire baseball games, or boating on the river.

Michael cleared his throat, "I'll come visit you, okay? We can come up with a plan to see each other as often as possible."

"Promise?"

"Of course. It's only two hours away and you know I love to drive."

Jenny smiled, despite her hurting heart. He probably wasn't any happier about her move than she was. But he was trying to be positive, for her sake.

Ugh. Michael was such a good guy. What if he found someone else while they were apart? What if he decided a long-distance relationship was too hard?

She wanted to pound her head against the steering wheel. Maybe she should consider turning down the job.

Before she could contemplate it any further, Michael spoke again. "You'll be an awesome Special Ed. teacher. And getting hired right out of college will look good on your resume."

"You're right. I'm excited, I really am." She sighed into the receiver. "It's just … I'll miss you. This has been the best summer of my life."

"Mine too." His voice sounded strained. It tugged at her heart.

She pressed harder on the gas and increased her speed. The sooner she arrived home, the more time she could spend with him before she had to say good-bye.

MICHAEL SLIPPED A LEI AROUND Jenny's neck, adjusting the yellow and pink flowers beneath her ponytail. After spending weeks apart, he soaked in every inch of her face—the pale pink color above her sea-blue eyes, the rose blush across her cheeks, the sparkly gloss highlighting her naturally tinted lips. "Aloha beautiful. Welcome to my Annual Rock-A-Luau Party."

Jenny gave him a weak smile and rested her head against his chest.

His eyebrows furrowed together. Something was wrong. In an effort to erase whatever was bothering her, he tipped her chin up to face him, dipped his head, and pressed his lips against hers. She melted into his kiss, a sense of desperation lingering between them for the weeks they'd spent apart. They'd seen each other several times over the last month, but only for a couple of days at a time. It was never long enough.

"Get a room, you two." Brian's voice came from a few feet away.

Michael pulled back slowly, not willing to pull his gaze away from Jenny just yet. She looked a little more at ease, but behind the light touches of makeup, he noticed dark lines below her eyes as if she hadn't slept well last night.

His gut hardened. What was bothering her?

Brian walked toward them, carrying a cardboard box full of eight small beanbags. "You guys up for a game of Cornhole?"

Jenny shook her head. "Maybe later."

Brian shrugged. "Scared to lose, huh? I get it. You'll have to face me at some point. These Luau's usually last all day."

Michael put his hands on his hips, keeping the conversation light. "You're on, man. We'll play the winners of the first game."

"Sweet." Brian walked away, approaching a group of their friends who were playing cards at the picnic table.

Jenny turned around. "I'll be back." With long, quick strides, she disappeared inside his house.

Michael swallowed hard. This was serious. Jenny was usually so laid back and carefree. He had to get to the bottom of this. He strode inside the house, catching the faint scent of her watermelon body soap. "Jenny?"

No answer.

He stopped in the living room, noticing the front door slightly open. He peered outside. Jenny sat hunched over on his porch, her elbows resting on her knees and her chin cupped in her hands.

Holding his breath, he stepped outside. A cool, fall wind rushed by, sending goose bumps up and down his arms. "Hey."

She glanced up at him, blinking back tears. "You didn't have to follow me. I don't want to ruin your Luau party."

His insides unraveled. "What's wrong?"

She picked up an orange leaf, twirling it between her fingers as a tear slipped down her cheek. "I can't do this anymore."

Michael sank down beside her. His heart raced in his chest, thudding so loudly it pulsated in his ears. "What do you mean?"

More tears ran down her face, falling onto her jeans. "I hate living away from you. And it's only going to get worse when you move. Then we'll be almost three hours apart."

This conversation was not headed in the right direction. He wouldn't lose her. He cared about her too much. "We can make this work. *I* want to make this work."

She looked up and met his gaze, her bottom lip quivering. "I do, too."

He smiled. At least she didn't want to break up. He put his hand on her knee. "Would you ever consider teaching in Iowa?"

Jenny stopped twirling the leaf, clearly caught off guard by his question.

He hated putting her in this position, but he couldn't imagine living without her. He wasn't just enjoying their time together, seeing where this relationship could go. He could see a future with her.

She rested her head on his shoulder. "It's crossed my mind lately. But my parents wouldn't be thrilled to have me so far away. And I'd need to find another job before I could move."

"My sister is a teacher in Davenport. She could put in a good word for you. And the Quad Cities has several other good school districts."

"You've put some thought into this, haven't you?" She leaned forward, a slight smile playing across her lips.

"Yeah, I have." Grinning, Michael cupped her face with his hands, gently rubbing the tearstains from her cheeks with his thumbs. "I love you, Jenny."

She blinked away a fresh set of tears. "I love you, too."

Hearing the words for the first time, his chest constricted. She loved him. He didn't need to know anything else. He leaned toward her, his lips barely brushing hers as he spoke with quiet assurance. "We will make this work."

JENNY DRAPED A TOWEL AROUND her shoulders as Michael drove his speedboat down the Mississippi River. The wind rippled past, whipping loose strands of hair across her sun-kissed face. She tucked them into her ponytail and pulled her shoulders back against the seat cushion, enjoying the warm summer rays caressing her cheeks.

Boating never got old. Since she'd moved to Bettendorf a month ago, they'd gone out on the river every weekend. With Michael's thriving business and long hours, some weeks it was the only time they spent together. He tried to visit her apartment other days, but after long hours of putting in irrigation systems, he needed to go home and rest.

Part of her felt a little lonely in this new city, but like a compass pointing north, moving closer to Michael felt right. And once school started in the fall, she'd be plenty busy with work and coaching.

Michael glanced over at her, raising his voice above the engine. "Want the radio on?"

She nodded, a smile tugging at her lips as he tapped his finger against wheel, singing along with "Life is a Highway." He exchanged a knowing look with her, remembering their first kiss.

Another speedboat drove past, and she turned her head in that direction. Could it be Michael's sister? She and her husband were supposed to meet them near a rope swing that hung from a huge tree along the shore, and they were getting close to it. But as she spotted the other boat, it carried a tube with giggling kids behind it. She stood and scanned the area, but no sign of his sister.

Michael slowed the boat, until they reached the tree and he let it idle above the waves. "We left a little early, so we might have to wait."

"That's fine." Jenny tossed her towel on the seat and retied the strings on both sides of her bikini bottoms.

His gaze traveled over her. "Want to know my favorite part about boating?"

"What's that?"

"Seeing you in a swimsuit." Her stomach dipped as he put both hands on her waist, pulling her closer until their hips touched. He still had an effect on her, much like the day he'd asked her to sit with him at the baseball game.

Grinning, she shook her head. "You're such a guy."

He shrugged and glanced at the river behind her shoulder. "I should warn you before my sister gets here … She's been a little persistent lately."

"About what?"

Michael scratched behind his head. "Well, she kinda likes you, and she thinks you're lonely in that apartment all by yourself."

A smile spread across her face. As much as she missed her own family, she enjoyed living near his sister and parents. His mom and sister asked her to go shopping and out to eat when Michael worked. On weekends, his parents often invited them over to dinner, and it melted her heart every time she saw Michael and his dad together. They were the cutest father-son duo, acting more like best friends. Now that she lived here, she could definitely see herself as part of his family. But she wouldn't press Michael on the issue; she'd let his sister do it for her.

Jenny put her palms on his chest. "Your sister is very intuitive. I'd listen to her if I were you."

He arched an eyebrow. "Oh yeah?"

"Just saying."

Chuckling, he ran his hands down her back, his fingers gently brushing over her bare skin. "It would be nice if we could spend more time together. I'd love to come home from work every day and we could have dinner, then spend the rest of the night hanging out. Without going back to our own places, I mean."

She bit back a smile. "Are you insinuating what I think you are?"

Michael nodded, his dark eyes lighting with excitement. "We could find a fixer-upper for a good price, and my dad and I could remodel it."

Squealing with delight, Jenny slipped her arms around his neck. The thought of a fixer-upper seemed overwhelming, but he'd already renovated a few houses that he now rented out, and those houses looked amazing.

And this time, he'd be working on *their* house.

She tilted her chin slightly and met his gaze. "It's an awesome idea."

A wide grin spread across his face, mirroring her own. For the first time since she'd met him, she had no doubt about one thing. She and Michael had a future together.

WHERE ARE THEY NOW?

JENNY AND MICHAEL HAVE BEEN MARRIED for seven years. Soon after Jenny moved to Bettendorf, they bought a fixer-upper and completely remodeled it. Last year, they bought a house in the same neighborhood as Michael's parents. They are currently renovating it one project at a time. They enjoy family activities with their young son and daughter, like boating, camping, and biking.

New Kind of Normal

Colorado Springs 2014

SARAH STOVER TRUDGED UP the sidewalk, stopping in front of a three-story beige brick house. Stuffing her hands inside her big puffy coat, she leaned back on her heels, soaking in the view. The Rocky Mountains rose above the hilly neighborhood with hazy purple mist blanketing the snow-covered peaks.

This was a view she could get used to.

A car door slammed shut and Arthur McManus walked toward her. Behind his thick glasses, his pale blue eyes lit with excitement. "I think you're gonna like this one."

Sarah gave him a weary smile. She should have bought another cup of coffee on her drive over, just to match Arthur's energy level. So far he'd shown her ten houses in the last five days, and every day, his energy seemed to increase.

Or maybe hers had deflated. Either way, house

hunting in Colorado Springs wasn't exactly what she had envisioned. No place seemed right. Maybe she was being too picky—this wasn't a forever home—but with the mountain of money sitting in her bank account, she had to purchase something sufficient. It was the right thing to do, wasn't it?

Arthur stopped next to her, running a hand over his gray five o'clock shadow. "What do you think of the exterior?"

Her gaze traveled over the house, carefully assessing every inch. "The blue trim is a little odd. I would definitely paint over it."

"This house needs some updates, but keep an open mind. It has potential."

"That's fine." A fixer upper would be the perfect opportunity to personalize the house, even if she moved out after she graduated with her master's degree. But she wouldn't worry about it now. Two years was a long way away and life could change in an instant.

She knew that better than anyone.

She glanced up at the mountains again, distracted by their magnificent beauty. "Now I get where Purple Mountain Majesty comes from."

"The view is even better from the backyard.

There's a big deck. Plenty of room for a table and chairs, even a grill."

Space for a grill—a must-have for Chris. Back when they'd started dating, he had made an offer on his first home. He'd taken her there that same day and showed her the open floor plan, the screened-in porch where he could brew beer, and the backyard, where there was space for a grill.

Sarah almost smiled at the memory. That night Chris had been so proud of his soon-to-be home. It was the perfect starter house, until the Air Force had stationed him in England.

Arthur cleared his throat. "Ready to check out the interior?"

"Sure." Sarah followed him up the inclined driveway, waiting on the porch as he fiddled with the key lock. She paced back and forth, just to stay warm. Spring weather in Colorado was definitely colder than she'd imagined. She'd have to grow another layer of skin while she lived here.

Arthur unlocked the door, its hinges groaning the farther it opened. He held out his arm, gesturing for her to enter.

She stepped inside, and her lips parted. Talk about a fixer-upper: gold hardware, popcorn ceilings, tan paint, and worn wood trim. This place would need *a lot* of work.

She shuffled forward, her gaze resting on a bay window overlooking the front yard. It had a big ledge, spacious enough for a doggy bed. "I bet Schrodie would love lying here. Carolina Dogs are shy, so at least he can see people on the street before he decides to hide from them."

Arthur snapped his fingers as if he'd just re-membered something. "Speaking of your dog, there's no fence."

"That's not a problem. Schrodie's well trained. When Chris and I lived in England, we'd take our dog for walks all the time and let him roam around without a leash." She slumped down to the ledge, her legs suddenly heavy. "It might take Schrodie some time to get used to city life again, but I'm sure he'll be fine."

If only she could say the same. Moving from the countryside back to the city would be a huge adjustment, one she wasn't ready for. Part of her longed to be back in England, but this was where she needed to be. For Chris' sake. And if she was being honest with herself, for her sake too.

Arthur sighed, the excitement in his eyes fading

a little. He must have taken her seated position in the window as a bad sign.

Sarah scooted off the ledge and walked into the living room, admiring the gas fireplace. "I've always wanted one of these." She ran her fingers along the mantel, her chest constricting. If only she could cuddle in front of the fire with Chris.

"Let me show you the rest of the house." Arthur showed her the kitchen, an office, the basement with a guest room, and the upstairs bedrooms. He let her linger in each space, giving her time to contemplate whether this house was the right fit. Every room needed updates, but most of them were cosmetic.

Her mind reeled with possibilities—the prospect both exciting and daunting. She'd have to change all the gold hardware, repaint the trim, and fix the ceilings, but it definitely had potential with space for studying, relaxing, and hosting guests. This was the best place she'd seen so far.

At the end of the tour, Arthur stepped out onto the back deck and leaned against the railing. His gaze rested on the mountains, even when he spoke to her. "What do you think?"

The question made her heart race, thudding so hard it would surely explode. She had to make a decision. Graduate school started in the fall and she would need to find a place before then. Buying a house felt so permanent. Maybe she could ask Arthur to show her more rentals.

And yet, after seeing this house, imagining the renovations, renting didn't feel right either.

But could this be *home*? Even unspoken, the word tasted bitter.

Arthur's eyebrows creased together, causing a wave of wrinkles to surface on his forehead. "Are you okay?"

Sarah ran a hand through her hair, planning to draw her long locks around her face like a veil, but she found short strands instead. She wasn't used to her new pixie cut.

"Excuse me." Turning, she sprinted through the house and dashed out the front, hopping into her Audi. Grabbing her GPS, she put in the address to Peterson Air Force Base. She couldn't make this decision alone.

She had to talk to Chris.

Georgia 2011, Three years earlier …

SARAH SNUGGLED CLOSER TO CHRIS, resting her head on his chest. His heart beat rhythmically against her ear, the sound so soothing it almost lulled her to sleep. She blinked, forcing her heavy eyelids to stay open. Sleeping would waste precious minutes of Chris' leave. Next week, the other side of the bed would be empty, and he'd be deployed to Afghanistan.

The thought of his absence made her chest tighten.

But at least they lived together now. A few months ago, during his deployment in Iraq, she'd moved in to his house. After dating for a year and spending most of it apart, she couldn't fathom the idea of living without him.

Chris massaged her scalp and ran his fingers through her long blond locks. "Did you have fun tonight?"

She nodded against his chest, replaying moments from the Squadron Party. "It's fun seeing everyone cut loose. And I really like Wendy, Evan's girlfriend. We plan on hanging out while you and Evan are deployed."

"Great. It'll be nice for you to have someone like

her in your support system. She knows exactly what you're going through."

Beneath the comforter, Sarah put her hand on his bare stomach, following the light trail of hair up to his chest. She wished she could understand what Chris went through, but she could only imagine— living in a foreign country, flying a helicopter during combat, picking up wounded soldiers—it sounded so terrifying. "Are you scared?"

"No, I'm trained to do my job. I look at deployments as opportunities to do just that."

"You're amazing, you know that? Most people wouldn't risk their lives on a daily basis."

He shrugged. "That's a big part of it, but I love flying. It's always been my dream to be a pilot, and in the Air Force I get a lot of time to fly."

Pride swelled in her heart. Chris knew of the risks, and he'd signed up for the Air Force anyway. He didn't talk about his experiences often, and she always wondered if anything scared him.

He turned over on his side, his dark brown eyes illuminated by the lamp on her nightstand. "If anyone's amazing, it's you. People don't give the loved ones enough credit. You're the one who's left behind worrying and wondering if I'm safe."

Adjusting her head on the pillow, she blinked again, this time to prevent tears from slipping down her cheeks. How sweet that he would hold her role to such high esteem.

But she had to admit that nothing could have prepared her for the military lifestyle. It took strength to love someone who wasn't always present because duty called him away. It took patience and faith to make it through deployments. It took tenacity to keep a relationship afloat, especially while they were still dating, with nothing permanent holding them together, aside from their growing love for one another.

Chris pushed up on his elbow, glancing over her shoulder at the alarm clock. "It's getting late."

"I don't want to go to sleep yet."

"Neither do I." He sat up, leaning his back against the headboard. He rubbed his crew cut, a restless expression crossing his downturned face.

Her stomach coiled. *Uh-oh.*

He stopped rubbing his head and met her gaze. "I have something I want to talk to you about."

"Okay." Sarah sat up too, draping her arms over her bent legs and waiting for him to continue.

"I've been contemplating this for a while now,

and I hope you don't think I'm crazy."

"What is it?"

A wide grin spread across his face. "I think you're the one for me."

She stared at him for a moment, her heart pounding as she processed what he'd just said. *He thinks I'm the one.* "I can't tell you how many times I've had that exact same thought."

His smile widened. "Then I hope you'll like my next idea." He reached for her hand, entwining their fingers as he spoke. "We could get engaged when I come back from Afghanistan. Your brother's getting married in July and that way there won't be any confusion on whether or not I should be in family pictures."

Tears welled up in her eyes. Chris was so practical, and yet, how romantic that he would care about being in family pictures at her brother's wedding.

"More importantly, I'd like to spend our early engagement days together."

Sarah leaned forward, put her hands on his chest, and knocked him down on the bed. "It's the best plan ever." She brought her lips to his, her heart expanding in her chest. She would surely explode with their secret, waiting for him to return from

Afghanistan.

No doubt she'd spend the next few months guessing how he would propose, where they would be, what he would say. And now that she knew, did that mean she could start planning the wedding—perusing through magazines for a wedding dress, choosing colors, making a list of possible venues?

She stopped her thoughts before they could go into full-fledged bride mode. They *weren't* engaged yet. She'd resist any wedding planning for now.

Besides, he could change his mind. He could come back from Afghanistan a changed man and not want to marry her.

Or worse, he might not come back at all.

Florida 2012

SARAH TIPPED HER HEAD BACK, finishing the last remains of her strawberry daiquiri. Licking her lips, she set the empty glass on the sticky counter and signaled for the burly bartender to get her another one. *Why not?* This relaxing vacation would only last a few days, and then she'd be back at work, wishing she could spend more time with Chris during his leave.

Unless … this wasn't just a relaxing vacation and Chris planned on proposing. They hadn't talked about it much during his deployment, but she'd replayed that conversation so many times it felt like a scene from a movie. Her excitement and doubts continued to plague her while he was gone, and she hoped with all her heart that he felt the same way now that he had back then.

The bartender set another daiquiri in front of her, and she chewed on her bottom lip. *Did* Chris have something more planned? If so, he'd surely be nervous, wouldn't he?

She glanced up at the beach bar TV, pretending to watch the hockey game and peeked at Chris out of the corner of her eye.

He was leaning back against the bar stool, wearing dark swim trunks that accented his lean, muscular stomach. He took a drink of his beer.

He didn't look nervous, so he probably wasn't planning on proposing just yet. Sarah reached her daiquiri, sipping the sugary concoction. She twisted her stool, swaying to the rhythm of the palm trees along the boardwalk.

Chris turned toward her, taking off his sunglasses and setting them above his dark hair. He wore a serious expression on his face, but his brown eyes held a glint of humor as he eyed her empty drink.

"What? Don't look at me that way. What happens in Florida, stays in Florida. I'm pretty sure that's how the saying goes, right?"

Chris kept a straight face for a moment longer before he broke into a grin. "Yeah, it's about *Florida*."

"That's what I thought. So don't judge." Sarah wagged her pointer finger close to his face, gently tapping his sun-kissed nose. She gave him a teasing smile; he was the least judgmental person she'd ever met—probably why she felt so comfortable being her quirky self around him.

"You want me to make you feel better?" Chris grabbed his beer, taking a long swig. Keeping his gaze locked on her, he finished the drink and wiped his mouth with the back of his hand.

"Thank you. I do feel better now." Giggling, Sarah leaned her head on his shoulder. The warm ocean breeze swept gently through the open bar. She hadn't felt this relaxed since Chris had left for Afghanistan. Being away from him was torture, as if someone had sucked all the oxygen from her body, leaving her without an air mask, gasping for breath.

But when they were together, all the worries, all the frustrations, floated away into some faraway land as if they never existed. Especially now that they were on vacation. Suddenly, she had more than enough air, so much that it left her giddy.

She wrapped her arms around Chris. "Thank you for planning this trip. I needed it so much."

"Me too." Chris put his hand above her knee, the calluses in his palm rough against her smooth legs. "We should head back to the room. Relax for a while before dinner."

She sat up straight, meeting his gaze and raised her eyebrows up and down. "Good idea."

Laughing at her insinuation, Chris reached for her hand, leading her away from the bar. They swung their arms as they strolled through the crowded boardwalk. A group of teenagers sat with their feet in the water, devouring tacos from one of the vendors. Two silver-haired men walked by, carrying fishing poles over their shoulders. A family of four brushed sand off their feet. Sarah smiled at the family. Maybe one day that would be her and Chris with their children.

They took their time making it back to the hotel and once they made it to their room, Chris opened the sliding glass doors. A warm breeze blew through the curtains. He stood in the doorway facing the bay with his hands in his pockets. "Check out this view."

She came up behind him, putting her arms around his trim waist. Resting her chin on his shoulder, she followed his gaze. The sun was setting below the horizon, and orange and pink hues were smeared across the sky like a watercolor painting. Down below, lights from restaurants showcased the lively boardwalk. "It's beautiful."

She walked around him and stepped out onto the porch. Plopping down in a white plastic chair, she patted the one next to her. "Care to join me?"

Chris tapped his lips. "Hmm, let me think about it."

She batted her eyelashes. "Puh-puh-please?"

"I don't know. Have you been good enough today?" A teasing grin spread across his face before he jumped into the empty chair, almost toppling it over.

Sarah giggled. "You're ridiculous."

"I'm going to take that as a compliment." Slipping out of his flip-flops, he pulled a plastic end table closer, resting his feet on top of it. Leaning back, he put his hands behind his head. "This is the life."

"Uh-huh." The effects from the drinks were slowly wearing off, making her eyelids feel heavy. She had to catch her second wind.

Tapping her fingers along the armrest, she tried to come up with a topic that would refuel her energy. *Work?* Definitely not. *Tomorrow's agenda?* Possibly. *Plans for the summer?* She did have something in mind that she hadn't mentioned to Chris yet. She sat up straighter, gently smacking his leg. "I have an idea."

Chuckling, he waved his hand, encouraging her to continue. "What is it?"

"You know how we have a long drive back home?"

"Yes, but why are you thinking about the end of our trip when it just started?"

"Because …" She paused for a moment, letting his anticipation rise as she pulled her windswept hair up into a messy bun. "What if we stopped at shelters on the way home and started looking for a dog?"

Chris' mouth fell open, his dark eyes sparkling in the fading sunlight.

"I know we haven't talked about it in a while, but last summer you said you wanted to wait until after you were back from Afghanistan." Sarah sat forward, bending her legs crisscross in the chair. "Well, it's after."

Grinning, he dropped his feet to the floor, bouncing his knees up and down. "I'd have plenty of time to help nurture and train the dog."

She rolled her eyes. "You're such a nerd."

Chris put a hand over his chest. "That hurts."

"Want to come up with some names, just in case we find *the one*?"

"Now, who's the nerd? We're talking about a dog."

She crossed her arms. "Hey, be respectful to the canines."

He laughed. "Okay, the name should be something smart. That way he or she can live up to the name." Chris' eyebrows creased together, deep in thought. "We could name him or her after a scientist."

She didn't bother to ask if he was joking. Once he had an idea in his head, there was no going back. Her mind reeled, trying to remember names of various scientists from her Gen. Ed. courses in college. "There's Newton … or Einstein."

"Or Copernicus."

"Wait." She held up her hand. "I want a short name or at least a name that can be shortened into a nickname."

"What about Tesla?"

"Oh, I like that for a girl. But what about a boy's name?" Sarah thought about the conversation they'd had about Schrodinger's cat, and she wildly flapped her hands in the air. "I've got it!"

He laughed. "What is it?"

"Since we already have a cat, we could name the dog Schrodinger, that way Izzie could literally be Schrodinger's cat." She lifted her chin and wiped her palms together, waiting for Chris' response.

He broke into a wide grin. "And we could call him Schrodie for short."

Sarah pumped her fist into the air. "Yes. I love it." She leaned over, her face close to his. "Not to be corny, but I love you too."

"There's nothing wrong with corny. Now that we have that figured out, do you want to get dinner?"

She nodded, a peaceful contentment floating through her. They were getting a dog. It finally felt like they were moving forward after so many months of stagnancy.

She started to pull herself up, but Chris put his hand over hers, grabbing her attention. "Before we go out to dinner, I have a question for you." He slid out of his chair and got down on one knee, reaching inside the pocket of his swim trunks. "I've been waiting all day for the perfect moment to do this."

Sarah sat frozen for a moment. Shock, guilt, and delight tugged at her emotions until she couldn't hold any of them back. Tears slipped down her cheeks. *Ugh*, he'd been waiting for her to get sober. Leave it to her to almost mess this up.

Chris pulled a sparkling princess cut diamond out of his pocket. She stared at the solitaire ring. It was simple and elegant and beautiful. More tears streamed down her face.

His Adam's apple bobbed up and down as he lifted the ring higher. His voice shook as he spoke. "Will you marry me?"

Her heart picked up speed, thrumming against her chest. Time seemed to slow down and pick up at the exact same moment, making it hard to concentrate. She mumbled something incoherent, and he reached for her hand, slipping the ring on her finger.

She lunged into his arms, crossing her ankles around his waist and pressing her lips against his.

Had she just said yes? She must have, and of course, she'd meant it with all her heart. It was a *yes* to being married to her best friend, and a yes to living a military lifestyle, knowing they could get stationed anywhere in the world, constantly wondering if Chris was safe, being alone for several months out of the year. It was all worth it.

England 2013

"SCHRODIE, LOOK OVER THERE—A CHICKEN COOP!" Sarah pointed across the open farmland, her wedding ring glimmering in the sunlight. They'd been married for almost a year, and it still shined like it was brand new.

Schrodie took off, his lean form galloping toward the community garden, where several chickens peeked through the iron fence. Seeing the big dog, the chickens let out high-pitched clucks.

Chris chased after Schrodie and glanced over his shoulder at her. "This open space is great for him."

She nodded. It was great for Chris too. England was his second station as a pilot, and right before he'd been assigned here to the 56th Rescue Squadron, he'd been promoted to Captain. She was so proud of him for meeting his goals, and when he'd told her about moving to England, she'd been thrilled. What could be more fun than traveling overseas with your partner in crime?

If only she felt that optimistic now that they were here. Their house in Red Lodge was almost empty, except for a mattress on the floor and several boxes of household items. Nothing could be put away until the rest of their luggage arrived.

Sighing, she surveyed the foreign land. A few yards away, a soccer field ran parallel to a cricket field, where a group of coeds played the game.

Chris jogged back to her, his eyebrows furrowing together above his sunglasses. "Is something wrong?"

She chewed on the inside of her cheek and met his gaze, trying to decide where to start. "It's been a hard day."

"We have a long walk to the onion patch. Tell me about it." He took a step forward, waiting until she moved beside him.

They walked side by side, watching Schrodie as he paced back and forth in front of the chicken coop. His tongue hung out, slobber dripping onto the plush green grass. Chris was right. The wide-open countryside was an easy adjustment for their dog. But it hadn't been for her, and she had to be honest with Chris about her feelings.

Sarah stuck her hands in the pockets of her jeans, looking down at the ground. "The last few days have been so long while you're at the base. There's nothing for me to do."

She tugged at her scarf, loosening the hold around her neck. She hated complaining, especially to Chris when he'd experienced much worse days. And yet, she needed to vent. "Transitioning from a full-time job to having no job is harder than I thought it would be. I mean, I thought I'd like the change of pace, but I feel so restless."

Chris nodded, his eyes full of understanding.

"I think it'll be easier when the rest of our stuff arrives. At least I can start organizing our house so it won't feel empty anymore."

"And when that's all done, you'll start school. I'm sure that'll keep you busy."

"That's true." Her Rhetoric and Writing Master's Program started in just a few months. No doubt her perfectionism would drive her into full-blown study mode. She could find a nice little coffee house and get lost in her books for the rest of the day. And after what happened today, she really needed to find a good coffee house.

Her lips drew into a thin line. "I have a confession."

Chris raised an eyebrow. "Go on, my dear," he spoke in a slow, deep tone, trying to sound like a priest.

"Not that kind of confession." Rolling her eyes, she gave him a playful push. "As you know, Schrodie woke me up early this morning. Feeling super tired, I filled the coffee pot—it still smells deliciously new and plastic, by the way—and I scooped ample amounts of Dunkin Donuts into the filter."

At the sound of his name, Schrodie's ears perked up and he strolled over, squeezing himself between them. His tail wagged against her legs, and she stopped, scratching behind his ears. "I turned the machine on and the deceptive power surge lit up and turned orange. I was practically salivating at this point."

Chris chuckled. "Deceptive, huh?"

"Yeah." Glancing up at him, she let out a frustrated growl. "Nothing happened. No water, no heat, no coffee."

"And no patience from a caffeine freak," he added.

"Exactly."

Chris crouched down, running his hand over Schrodie's back. "I'm scared to ask, but what did you do?"

"I did what any sane American would do." She bit back a smile. "I swore at it."

He grinned. "Yes, that makes perfect sense. I'm sure the coffeemaker responded well to your uplifting words."

"You would think so, but no. But I did the next best thing." She dug her boot into the hard ground. "I kicked it."

He stopped petting Schrodie. "No you didn't."

"Yup, I moved it from the counter to the floor, and then I kicked it." Sarah let out a giggle, feeling much lighter after telling him. "I couldn't help it. I was so mad."

"Yeah, I caught that part." Chris shook his head, running a hand over his clean-shaven face. "Did you ever figure out what the problem was?"

"Yeah. The 110 volt coffeemaker that I smartly plugged into the adapter had burnt out the heating element after one use. Appliances here are 220 volt. Our adapter only converts the plug, not the voltage."

"Ah, that makes sense." He was quiet for a moment, most likely contemplating how to make her feel better. Whenever she was upset, he seemed to take her burden as if it were his own, trying to find a solution.

He held out his hand. "Come here." He gently pulled her down to the ground until they sat side by side. Leaning over, he kissed her cheek.

The gesture brought a calming contentment settling through her body like a relaxing day at the beach.

Kissing her cheek again, Chris met her gaze. "Living here will get better, I promise. We'll settle into the house, we'll go for long runs in the countryside, we'll take day trips around England, we'll make new friends—it'll be our new normal."

Normal. It all felt so foreign right now, but he was probably right. He had such a way of keeping her grounded. She leaned her head on his shoulder.

"I'm sorry. I really am excited about this new chapter of our lives. I just lost sight of the adventure for a moment. Thanks for reminding me."

"Of course," he said, resting his head against hers.

Chris was right. Things hadn't been that bad. Their lease had ended right as Chris' deployment started in England, so they hadn't had to make two house payments. The trip to England had been a blast, and both Schrodie and Izzie did well, considering they'd traveled for almost five days and over four countries.

His lips curled into a mischievous grin. "I have a confession to make too."

"That smile is dangerous. What did you do?"

"Remember when we talked about getting new seat covers for our car?"

"You bought some?"

"That's not the best part. They're hot pink."

Giggling, she slapped her leg. Leave it to Chris to do something no one would ever expect. But there was one little problem. "You won't believe this, but so did I."

He laughed. "No way."

"Yes way." She turned toward him completely

and hopped into his lap. Putting her hands behind his head, she pressed her forehead against his. "How can we *not* have fun living here if we're driving around with hot pink seat covers?"

"That's the spirit, darling." Chris laughed at his attempted English accent; it sounded more Australian.

Either way, it sounded sexy coming out of his mouth. She ran her fingers over his short hair and trailed kisses from his chin to his cheeks, to his nose, to his forehead. His hands caressed her back, diminishing the last remnants of her frustration.

The day's events seemed so trivial now. Everything would be okay. She had Chris, and he was all she needed.

Colorado Springs 2014

THE COLD SPRING AIR STUNG Sarah's face as she walked past the iron gates of the Air Force Academy Cemetery. Trees were scattered across the cemetery, their bare branches sprouting tiny pink buds.

Maneuvering through the graves, questions

probed her mind like needles puncturing her skin. Could she really buy the house? She yearned to ask Chris for advice. He was always better at seeing the big, financial picture.

She picked up her pace, her breathing growing rapid when she spotted Chris' grave. She dropped to her knees, running her fingers over his name. *I miss you more than words can express. Four months without you and it feels like I lost you yesterday.*

Hot tears slipped down her cheeks, her stomach coiling with guilt. The only reason she could purchase a house was because Chris was gone. His death gave her the financial stability to buy a house. It didn't seem right to have any stability when Chris wasn't here. She should be experiencing this with him, not because of him.

With a shaky hand, she continued to trace the letters on his grave until her fingers stopped frozen above the last words. *That Others May Live.* Anger boiled within her, seething like lava beneath a volcano. So often people worshipped the valor or honored the sacrifice, but they failed to acknowledge the cost—the cost of a soldier's life, of Chris' life.

On January 7th, shortly after they'd moved to England, Jolly 22 went down, killing four crew members. During a preparation training flight along the marshlands coastline, multiple geese caused the accident by striking the windshield, rendering Chris unconscious. The helicopter crashed within seconds, leaving no time for the other crew members to react.

Part of her felt relieved that he hadn't died in the midst of combat, and yet, why did he have to die in training?

Sarah pounded her fist into the ground at the injustice. She'd found that perfect treasure, only to lose it at sea, somewhere so deep no one could touch it. She'd been robbed of the goodness they were building, of the special bond they shared as not only husband and wife, but as best friends.

She slumped forward, setting her forehead on his grave. Somehow, she felt closer to him this way. Losing Chris felt like an amputation—an extension of herself was gone. Missing him would always feel like hell. But the most difficult part of losing Chris was dealing with the flutters of hope, believing that this was just another deployment. Thinking, for a brief moment, that he would come home and everything would be okay. When it happened, it left her deflated, like a balloon contracting back to a wrinkly, withered version of her former self.

She would never be the same.

Life was still happening—it simply lacked the brilliance and warmth it once held. She wouldn't let her grief stop her. She wasn't afraid of her sadness. Perhaps a little tired of it, but not afraid. The worst had already happened; there wasn't much left to fear.

She had no idea what normal was anymore. She would trade anything to stand in the galley kitchen of their England home, swearing at a coffeemaker just to hear Chris tell her everything would be all right.

Relearning happiness would take time and strength. For her impatient heart, it felt like an eternity. Loving him came so easily. The happiness and love he brought into her life humbled her deeply. She'd honestly wondered how people got that lucky.

Sarah closed her teary eyes, picturing Chris on their wedding day—his navy uniform that fit snugly over his shoulders, the dark bow tie he'd insisted on wearing, his bright, clean-shaven face, and his big, genuine smile.

Her chest constricted, yearning to hold him, kiss him, and hear his voice. She opened her eyes before the magnitude of her grief could pull her under. Pulling herself up, she sat cross-legged in the grass. She tugged at a few blades, absentmindedly pulling them out of the ground.

As the fresh green grass slid through her fingers she remembered the night that Chris had showed her his house in Georgia, and she'd taken off her shoes, sliding her bare feet over the plush, vibrant ground. He'd been so excited to make that place his first home.

Sarah plucked several more strands of grass out of the ground, asking the same question she'd thought of earlier. Could the fixer-upper be her home? She sighed, her breath forming in front of her face. She needed a new normal, but she didn't want it.

She tilted her head back, letting the sunlight caress her cheeks. "What should I do, Chris? Should I put an offer on the house?"

She didn't expect an answer, but it felt good to ask him anyway, as if he was still a part of her decision.

Light snowflakes descended from the sky, spiraling through the bitter cold. Her eyes widened. *No way.* On the day of Chris' funeral, a beautiful pristine snow had covered the academy. Not so strange, except it had been in the 50s the day before. Following the funeral, she'd flown out to Vancouver for a memorial run in honor of Chris. The day of the run, it had snowed, and snowed, and snowed.

Chris loved the snow. He enjoyed making fun of her when she put on multiple layers of clothes just to thwart the cold temperatures.

Was this a sign to buy the house?

A smile tugged at her lips. Of course it was. She tilted her head back, appreciating the wet cold snowflakes for the first time, and savoring the perfect reminder that Chris was not so far away, after all.

Some sentences and phrases were taken from Sarah's blog: thatothersmaylove.blogspot.com

WHERE ARE THEY NOW?

SARAH LIVES IN COLORADO SPRINGS. She graduated with her Master of Arts in Clinical Mental Health Counseling in May of 2016. She works for the VA as a Licensed Professional Counselor Candidate. It's her own way of living the mission That Others May Live. She loves exploring local craft breweries, hiking, and continues to run races from 5ks to marathons. She still thinks of Chris every time it snows and every time she sees a rainbow.

FINALLY

LYRA JOHNSON PULLED BACK THE CURTAIN, peeking at the crowd. Parents and students stood in the bleachers, clapping and whistling for her cast of student actors. One by one, Gaston, Belle, and Beast walked to the middle of the gym floor and bowed, just like they'd practiced.

She smiled and let go of the curtain. The students had done such a great job, especially for a junior high play. No one had forgotten a line. The cast's enchanting rendition of "Be Our Guest" brought the audience to their feet. Gaston's natural charm had a few teenage girls practically swooning in their seats. Even costume issues weren't a problem. Beast's mask had never fallen off, and Lumière's candlesticks had stayed glued to his hands. Tonight's performance had gone much more smoothly than last night's.

Peter stopped beside her, microphone in hand.

"There's one person we forgot to thank. We need to say something."

"Really?" Lyra glanced up at him, mentally running through the list of people she'd already thanked before the performance. She couldn't think of anyone she'd forgotten. But Peter had orchestrated the songs and choreography for the show, so maybe he wanted to mention someone who had helped him.

She could also take this opportunity to address the students again. They deserved every bit of recognition. Hopefully, they were proud of themselves. Memorizing lines and singing in front of three hundred people took a lot of guts.

On stage, Belle and Beast clasped hands and took one final bow. The crowd erupted with applause. Two of the cast members turned in their direction, then quickly looked away, giggling.

Lyra stared at them for a moment. *What was that about?* The students probably thought Peter was flirting with her. This group of seventh and eighth grade girls were so boy crazy, always asking if any of the young teachers were dating. But then again, they knew Peter was married and she'd talked about Ryan plenty of times, enough for the students to know she was in a serious relationship.

Peter put a hand on her back, gently nudging her forward. "Let's go," he whispered.

She walked beside him to the middle of the makeshift stage, turning to face the audience. Close behind her, students stifled more giggles. Heat crept up the back of her neck. She lifted her dark loose curls and held them against her head for a moment, fanning her neck. If only she could ask them what was so funny, but the crowd grew silent, waiting for Peter to speak.

He flipped the microphone on with his thumb, and his calm, melodic voice carried through the gym. "There were so many wonderful volunteers who helped us this year, and one of those volunteers would like to speak to you."

What? That's not what he'd said backstage. Lyra let go of her curls. She shot her head in his direction as the overhead lights followed him off stage and he handed the microphone to someone.

Ryan stepped out from behind the curtain, tugging at the collar of his red button-down shirt. His hand moved from his shirt up to his honey blond hair, which was styled with a side part. As he walked forward, the stage lights illuminated the dark red blush accenting his pale, clean-shaved cheeks. "Hello everyone. My name is Ryan VanLanduyt."

Her jaw dropped open. There could only be one reason Ryan would get on stage and speak in front of an audience.

She waved her hands frantically in front of her face, trying to cool down and stay composed as he stepped closer, taking slow, deliberate strides.

Keeping his gaze locked on her, his blue-green eyes sparkled with mischief. He stopped in front of her, his lips curling up at one side in a shy, sexy grin. No doubt he was proud of himself for surprising her. She'd been giving him subtle hints about getting engaged for over a year.

"Lyra, I fell in love with your brilliance, your passion for life, and your thoughtfulness."

She clasped her hands over her mouth. *OMG. This was really happening.*

Ryan reached into the back pocket of his beige dress pants. He pulled out a shiny white-gold ring with two thin bands that curved together to meet a cushion cut diamond. The ring shook in his hands.

She held back a sympathetic grin. He had to be so nervous in front of all these people, but he'd planned a public proposal anyway, knowing how much this night would mean to her.

He let out a breath before speaking again. "And like the beast in the play tonight, I have found my beauty."

Blinking back tears, she pulled her hands away from her mouth, setting them over her ample chest. Her heart was beating so loud she could barely concentrate on what he'd just said. Hopefully, someone was recording this so she could replay it later.

Ryan bent down on one knee and lifted the ring, placing it close to her hands. His fingers trembled. "Lyra Johnson, will you marry me?"

She gazed down at him, a whirlwind of memories flooding back: forming a friendship in high school; flirting as coworkers at Hy-Vee Grocery; dating during college; spending time with their families; falling deeper and deeper in love with every new season of life.

Excitement bubbled in her chest. She gave several fervent nods, sending loose curls bouncing across her shoulders. "Yes, yes, yes."

Standing, a wide smile spread across Ryan's face. He put his arms around her and she sank into him, her head resting against his chest. Pulling back slightly, she cupped his face and stood on her tiptoes, bringing her lips to his for a sweet, slow kiss.

He'd seriously just proposed. After five years of dating, they were finally engaged. She could start planning their wedding. She waited for reality to settle in, but it felt too surreal. She'd thought about this moment so many times, wondering how he'd propose. But she never would've guessed it would be at the first show she ever directed, in front of all these parents and students. It was absolutely perfect.

Ryan VanLanduyt scrolled through the Christmas playlist on Lyra's phone, clicking on "Rudolph the Red Nosed Reindeer." Setting her phone back on the kitchen counter, he pranced into the living room of their apartment, maneuvering around boxes stuffed full of decorations.

Lyra hung a penguin ornament on the tree and turned around, catching sight of him. Beneath the white fluffy rim of her Santa hat, she rolled her eyes. "Oh no, you're dancing already? Did you put Captain in your hot chocolate?"

"No. Thank you very much." Living with Lyra

had brought out a different side of him, a goofy side that was often hidden in public. He put a hand on his chest, holding back a smirk. "I'm offended you would ask. Thankfully, I know a way you could make it up to me."

She put her hands on her hips and glared at him, sending a *don't even think about it* look.

She looked way too cute, trying to act tough like that. And standing a full foot shorter than him, her glare and stern posture did very little to stop him. He held out his hand, palm up. "My lady."

She crossed her arms over her black Hogwarts of Wizardry T-shirt, but her dark brown eyes held a glint of humor.

"Come on, you can't resist me for that long." He swayed his hips from side to side in big, dramatic motions.

Lyra smiled, the reflection of the Christmas tree lights reflecting off of her braces. She quickly covered her mouth.

He pulled her hand away. "Don't do that. You have a great smile." A few weeks after he'd proposed, she had braces put on. Her teeth had always made her self-conscious, and she wanted them to be straight for the wedding. He understood, so they'd set a date a few weeks after her braces would be taken off. A two year engagement wasn't a timeline either of them had wanted, but she deserved to feel as beautiful as she really was.

"Up on the Housetop" floated through the apartment. Lyra met his gaze, giggling. "Why not?"

"That's more like it." A wide grin spread across his face as they waltzed across the small, open apartment. The holidays would be so much fun. Lyra's mom and grandma always made a big fiesta meal with the most delicious tostadas he'd ever tasted. His brothers and their wives planned on flying in from out of state, and they usually planned a few bowling nights with their parents. And now that they lived together, he and Lyra could host a few family game nights as well.

The music stopped playing, replaced with vibrations from Lyra's phone.

She let go of his hand and twirled into the kitchen, picking up her cell. "Hi, Mom. What's up?"

Ryan reached for a string of silver garland, heading toward the tree. Lyra could be a while. She and her mom always found something to talk about— her brother's new job, her youngest sister's boyfriend, and with six months until the wedding, they loved discussing bridal showers and reception decorations.

"What's wrong?" Lyra's sharp tone sliced through the silence.

He turned around as she paced back and forth across the kitchen, clutching the phone to her ear as if it would slip out of her grasp. "Do you want us to come to the hospital?"

The blood drained from his face. *Hospital?*

"Give me a call as soon as you see a doctor." She slipped her phone inside the back pocket of her jeans and stared at the floor, appearing deep in thought.

His eyebrows furrowed together. "What's going on?"

"This morning when my mom woke up, she was puffy and swollen all over. It's gotten worse throughout the day, so she's going to the ER to get checked out."

"Do you think it's serious?"

"I don't know. She's been really sick with a bad cold all month." Lyra took slow steps into the living room and sank onto the couch. "Maybe she's having an allergic reaction to the cold medicine."

"Maybe." But he highly doubted it. Kathleen was a nurse and would surely know the signs of an allergic reaction. He wouldn't share his thoughts out loud, though; he didn't want to worry her.

Lyra took off the Santa hat and tossed it on the carpet. "There's no use trying to figure out what's wrong. I'm sure my mom will call back soon."

"Yeah, that's true." He tried to keep his voice light, but his lungs constricted making it hard to speak.

"Let's keep decorating." Lyra pushed herself off the couch and grabbed a small box of glittery green ornaments. She methodically placed each ornament on the tree, her shoulders drooping lower with every passing minute.

He cracked his knuckles. Kathleen had to be fine. It was probably a fluke reaction, caused by some coincidental circumstance. And yet, what if it *was* serious?

He shouldn't think like that, not without knowing the facts. He circled the thick tree, laying the silver garland on every few branches. The Christmas playlist resumed, and he hummed along, trying to lighten the mood and distract Lyra.

Vibrations buzzed from her phone again. She

exchanged a nervous glance with him before accepting the call and pressing *speaker*. "What did you find out?"

Seconds passed by before Kathleen spoke quietly into the receiver. "The doctor thinks I have leukemia."

His gut hardened. Kathleen couldn't have cancer. They'd just seen her last week when they were over for dinner, devouring her homemade enchiladas. She'd had a dry cough and runny nose, but that was it. The doctor must have made a mistake.

"Are you there?" Kathleen asked.

Blinking, Lyra stared at him as if she didn't really see him anymore.

He reached for her free hand, squeezing it. "Talk to your mom."

Lyra lifted the phone closer to her mouth. "I'm here," she croaked.

"They're rushing me to the local hospital."

"We'll meet you there." Lyra clicked off the phone, a mixture of emotions playing across her face: disbelief, worry, and mostly fear.

Pushing his own fears aside, he wrapped his arms around her, his protective instincts driving him into motion. She nestled her head against his chest, a soft sob escaping from her throat. Cupping the back of her head, he ran his fingers through her dark curls. "It's going to be okay."

As soon as the words tumbled out, he knew he shouldn't have said them. He wanted to make Lyra feel better, but if Kathleen had leukemia, he couldn't guarantee that everything would be all right.

LYRA KNOCKED ON THE HOSPITAL DOOR, trying to push away the guilt. She knew her mom had been sick but not *that* sick. If only she had paid more attention, but she'd been so preoccupied with wedding planning that she hadn't realized the full extent of her mom's illness.

"Come in." The quiver in her dad's voice was unmistakable.

Ryan opened the door for her, and she stepped inside, sucking in a rapid breath. Her mom lay in bed, her head propped up with a stack of white pillows as tubes snaked in and out of her nose and hands. Her face and arms were so inflated she looked like Violet after she'd chewed a bad piece of bubble gum from the Willy Wonka factory. But unlike Violet, her mom's coffee-colored skin appeared stark white and her lips were puffy and swollen.

She tore her gaze away, glancing at her dad. He sat beside the hospital bed, running a hand through his thin black and gray speckled hair. His bottom lip quivered. "Hey sweetie."

"We made it as fast as we could." Lyra reached for Ryan's hand, entwining their fingers. He squeezed her hand back, reminding her that he would stay right by her side.

Hannah dashed across the room, flinging her arms around Lyra's neck. Holding her youngest sister, moisture pressed against her eyelids, threatening to overflow. She blinked them away, unwilling to cry. She had to be strong for her sister. Being a sophomore in high school was hard enough.

"I'm so glad you're here." Hannah's voice sounded muffled against her sweatshirt.

Her sister pulled back slightly, and she wiped the mascara-stained tears running down her sister's cheeks, then walked to the hospital bed and sat down beside her mom. Above the bed, bright fluorescent lights illuminated her mom's face, their harsh glare revealing the dark circles beneath her heavily lidded eyes.

"Has the doctor told you anything yet?" Ryan asked.

Her mom let out a deep, throaty cough. She made a fist and covered her mouth, then sunk deeper into her pillow, putting a hand over her forehead. "No, but she should be back with the test results soon."

Lyra's chest constricted. Her mom looked awful, much worse than she had imagined. Tears threatened to break free again, but she blinked them away.

"I feel like death."

Lyra crossed her arms. "Don't say that, Mom."

"But I do. I've never felt this terrible in my entire life. It's like a darkness is hovering over me."

Could her mom be serious? She wasn't typically a dramatic person, but to *feel* darkness? What did that even mean? Lyra glanced at Ryan to get his reaction.

Meeting her gaze, his eyebrows furrowed together and his lips drew into thin line. He draped an arm around her shoulders. The comfort of his touch warmed her heart, if only slightly. He looked just as worried as she felt, but he was staying strong for her.

Three raps sounded on the door before a tall black-haired woman walked into the room. Her heels click-clacked against the vinyl floor until she stopped beside the hospital bed, clutching a clipboard against her long white coat. "Hi Kathleen. I'm Doctor Patel."

Her mom pushed a button on the remote, setting the bed at a higher incline. Somehow, she looked even paler than before. "What's the news?"

Doctor Patel took off her glasses, sliding them up over her forehead and resting them above her head. Wrinkles extended like webs from her dark eyes as she focused on Lyra's mom.

Lyra chewed on the inside of her cheek, waiting for an answer. A heavy sinking sensation settled at the bottom of her stomach like a big, metal anchor. If the doctor had a hard time speaking, this couldn't be good. Ryan broke the little amount of space left between them, holding her close to his side.

Her mom coughed, then cleared her throat. "Give it to me straight. Don't sugar coat it."

"Okay." Doctor Patel pressed the clipboard against her chest, clutching it so hard her knuckles turned white.

Lyra resisted the urge to cover her ears. Part of

her didn't want to know, as if that could somehow change the test results. She squeezed her eyes shut for a moment. *Please don't have cancer. Please don't have cancer.*

"You have acute leukemia."

Lyra's eyes flew open.

Doctor Patel lifted her chin. Red blotches traveled from her cheeks down her neck. "Your white blood cell count is over 1800."

Lyra's mouth went dry. She looked from the doctor to her mom, trying to get a read on the situation. But her mom sat as still as a mannequin, unblinking. How bad was a white blood cell count over 1800? Was it curable?

She opened her mouth to ask, but no words came out. Her throat felt like it had cotton balls stuck in it.

"What does that mean exactly?" her dad asked.

"1800 is a very high number. I've only seen one other case where the count was this high."

"What happened?" Her mom's voice trembled with fear.

"The patient passed away." Doctor Patel glanced down at her feet, speaking softly. "We'll start chemotherapy on Monday." She bit her bottom lip.

"But in all honesty, you might not make it through the weekend."

Lyra gasped, her breathing growing rapid. Her chest rose and fell. The walls caved in and she gulped for air, but all of it had left the room. How could this happen?

Her mom couldn't die. She was only fifty and still had a lot of living to do. She had to be at their wedding; she had to see if her brother, Elijah, met the girl of his dreams; she had to be there when Kira and Hannah graduated from high school. And that was just the beginning. Her brother and sisters would get married one day, and they would all start their own families. No doubt her mom would be an amazing grandma.

But Doctor Patel's words hung in the air like a heavy fog. *You might not make it through the weekend.*

Lyra's chest ached with excruciating pain. How much longer did her mom have? Hours? Days? A week at best?

RYAN GRIPPED THE STEERING WHEEL as he exited

the hospital parking lot. Snowflakes stuck to the windshield. The wind must have picked up in the last couple of hours. Turning on the windshield wipers, he glanced at Lyra.

She leaned forward in her seat, covering her face with her hands. She remained silent for a moment before quiet sobs escaped from her throat and her shoulders shook.

His heart hurt for Lyra and her family. They were so close. Sure, they had arguments and disagreements, but they loved spending time together, cooking authentic Mexican food at her grandma's house, buying a Christmas tree on Thanksgiving, playing card games. Family get-togethers would not be the same without Kathleen.

Lyra lifted her head, her red-rimmed eyes blood-shot and watery. "We should've gotten married sooner. Now, my mom won't be there." She let out a low growl. "I can't imagine getting married without my mom."

"I know. I can't either." He took one hand off the steering wheel and rested it on her thigh. "But she's a fighter. If anyone can survive this, it's your mom."

She gave him a weary smile. "What would I do

without you?"

His Adam's apple bobbed up and down. Her question was meant to be lighthearted, but with Kathleen's life in jeopardy, it left a hollow feeling in his gut. He wouldn't want to live a day without Lyra.

Pressing on the brakes, he pulled over to the side of the street and put the car in park.

"What are you—?"

He cut off Lyra's question, leaning over the middle console and pressing his lips against hers. She was hesitant at first, but then she moved closer, deepening the kiss. He felt her relax just a bit as she poured all of her emotions—her anxiety, fear, pain—into the kiss. No one knew what the future would bring, but at least for this moment, they had each other.

Six Months Later …

LYRA STOOD IN THE LOBBY of St. Anne's, just outside the open chapel doors. Her flowing white dress moved each time she fidgeted. The pianist paused for dramatic effect before she struck the first chord to "Canon in D."

People shuffled in the pews, standing to face her. She linked arms with her dad and took a step forward, her crochet Toms making contact with the center aisle. *Don't look down, don't look down* she reminded herself.

She bit her bottom lip and glanced up, catching sight of her mom's radiant face in the front pew. A wide smile spread across Lyra's face as she soaked in every inch of her mom's outfit—silver sandals, a sparkly knee-length silver dress, and a long dark wig.

How many sleepless nights had she spent wondering if her mom would still be alive today? After several rounds of chemotherapy, her mom had beat the odds. She still didn't feel like her old self, but day-by-day, she was growing stronger and healthier. It was truly a miracle.

Lyra winked at her mom, then turned her attention to the end of the aisle. Ryan stood with his hands clasped in front of him. His charcoal gray tuxedo fit crisply across his shoulders and lean torso. Like the day he'd proposed, his honey blond hair lay neatly styled in a side-part, accenting his square jaw line.

With every step, her heart swelled. Ryan looked undeniably handsome, suave even. She felt so lucky to be his. He had been her rock the last six months—drying her tears, listening to her worries, encouraging her to stay positive. After everything they'd been through, she knew with certainty he would be the perfect partner.

Stopping in front of him, her dad kissed her cheek and shook hands with Ryan, leaving the two of them facing each other on the altar in front of Father Charles.

Ryan reached for both of her hands, his eyes glistening. "You look like an angel with all the lights shining down on you," he whispered.

She blinked back joyful tears. He was the sweetest man she knew. "Thank you."

Father Charles started the sermon, his calm, confident disposition captivating the audience. Several women fanned themselves with programs. Some of them were blushing and it wasn't because of the heat. Father Charles had that effect on women. But not Lyra. Not with the perfect groom standing right next to her.

Near the end of the ceremony, Father Charles stood at the middle of the altar. He directed the vows, then clasped his hands together. "It is now time for the couple to exchange their wedding rings."

Turning, Ryan took the ring from his best man and slid it past her pale pink fingernail up to the top of her finger. His touch sent tingles up and down her arms. His voice remained low and steady as it resounded through the chapel. "I, Ryan, take this ring as a sign of my love and fidelity. In the name of the Father, the Son, and the Holy Spirit."

Lyra swallowed hard and repeated the blessing. Her maid of honor handed her Ryan's ring, and she slid it onto Ryan's finger.

Father Charles held out his arms, a wide smile spreading across his face. "I now pronounce you husband and wife."

Lyra's heart raced with the finality of those words. Ryan was finally her husband. They could spend the rest of their lives together, making memories. They could buy a house. Start a family. See the world together. The possibilities were endless.

Ryan put his arms around her lower back, his eyes hungrily devouring her face. Standing on her tiptoes, she swung her arms around his neck. He lifted her off the ground, his face moving closer until their lips met. They'd only planned on a sweet kiss in front of all their friends and family, but now that the moment was here, she surrendered to the flames engulfing them, enjoying the tantalizing kiss.

After all, life couldn't always happen the way she planned. Sometimes, it worked out better.

WHERE ARE THEY NOW?

LYRA AND RYAN HAVE BEEN MARRIED for two years. They recently bought a house and adopted a puppy, who they treat like a baby … but not for long. They recently announced that they are pregnant. Lyra's mom is still in remission and has gone back to work as a nurse. Ryan and Lyra are excited for her to be a grandmother, and they can't wait to see what the future will bring.

AUTHOR'S NOTE

Dear Reader,

A few years ago if someone had told me I'd publish short stories about real couples, I would've laughed. At the time, I was working on a romance novel. I rarely read nonfiction and I preferred novels compared to short stories. But the idea for this collection jumped into my head and then kept tugging at my heart. Stories based on real couples. Flawed, everyday people like you and me, who hope they have found the love of a lifetime.

Each couple featured in this book has laid it all out there for you, exposing their inner thoughts and emotions as they decided if their relationships were worth pursuing.

It was so much fun meeting with couples, hearing what they remember. Some people recall exactly what was said, others remember every emotion they felt, and some people can describe a setting so well it's like they have a permanent picture engraved in their minds.

A lot of people have asked me if I know the couples. I have met some of them. I was at the play when Ryan proposed to Lyra. It was the best proposal I've ever seen, besides my own. I knew Mary and Daniel before they were divorced, but I had no idea that Daniel battled with alcoholism. I hope one day he will recover. I first wrote "Uncharted Territory" as Tony's surprise anniversary present to Steph. It was quite nerve-racking to write a love story with only one person's perspective, especially the guy's point of view (they seem to remember details differently than women). A fun fact about Tony and Steph is that their son is Caleb Liston, who is featured in *Completely Captivated*. Whether I have met the couple or not, I enjoyed "spending time inside their heads" as they fell in love with their significant others.

I hope you were captivated by these stories— laughed a bit, smiled a lot, felt your heart pounding with emotion as you discovered who would end up brokenhearted and who would find their lifetime love. And now that you've finished the book, I hope you appreciate even more the beauty of love, despite its messy complications.

If you have a minute, please consider leaving a review. I remember the first review I received on *Completely Captivated.* I printed it and framed it. It's exciting to hear what readers think. Every review means so much to me. Your words are powerful, and I thank you in advance for taking the time to write your thoughts.

Love,
Crystal

ACKNOWLEDGMENTS

When I was in fourth grade, I decided to be an author.

And then I tried to talk myself out of it. What kind of life could an author have? I imagined sitting in a dark office, the only light coming from my computer screen; an almost silent house, except for the rhythmic sounds of typing; and being so, so alone in my weird writing world.

It's a good thing I never talked myself out of it. I was *so* wrong! Authors don't live in quiet solitude. In fact, I'm grateful for all of the encouraging family and friends who accept my writer weirdness.

A special thank-you to the people who make the writing life much more loud and colorful than I ever imaged:

Mike, my husband—I know your analytical brain doesn't understand the joy I get from brainstorming plots and crafting characters, but I appreciate when you listen to my ideas. It was so sweet of you to make those Excel spreadsheets for my books … if only I knew how to analyze them.

My sweet darlings—my heart swells with so much love for the two of you, even when you toss Play-Doh in my coffee and put Cheetos in my hair.

Mom, "my career manager"—I look forward to hearing about the new readers you meet almost every day. They are so lucky to receive a copy from you, especially when they get an earful of your Sandy-ness too. I don't know what I'd do without you.

Dad—I was so boy-crazy growing up. I'll never forget how you held me in your arms while I sobbed over my first boyfriend, but you always encouraged me to keep dating. I'm glad I took your advice; now I can use all those experiences in my stories!

All four of the kids' grandparents—this book would still be sitting in my computer if it weren't for you. The kids might not understand what it means when "Mommy leaves to work on her books," but they *do* know they're getting more time with their grandmas and grandpas.

Janice, my critique partner—even though we live states apart now, I'm so excited we're experiencing this publication journey together. I wouldn't want anyone else in the passenger seat, helping me navigate.

All the couples who submitted love stories—without you, this book would not be possible. You opened your hearts by sharing the most intimate thoughts and emotions from your relationships. Readers are forever blessed to read your touching stories.

Jeane Wynn, my publicist—I've really enjoyed working with you. Your knowledge and expertise is undeniable. Thank you for believing in me.

Mandie Leytem and Jen Tucker—girls, your friendships mean so much to me. I wish we lived closer, but your phone calls leave me smiling every time. Thank you for your constant encouragement and support, and thank you for being amazing friends.

Ben Hoffman—I love discussing writing with you.

Your perspective is always unique, and you offer great feedback when I ask … and even when I don't. Keep writing!

Erika Pickering—oh Mama-dear, I look forward to our frequent play dates. Sometimes, you are the only adult I talk to during the day, and you make me feel human.

Ann Martin, Stephanie Liston, and Sheri Zeck—thank you for reading the first draft. Your insight and suggestions added a glimmer to this book that wasn't there before.

Lisa Kimbrough and Nicole Thomason—we don't see each other often enough, but when we do, we always pick up right where we left off. I'm blessed to have you both.

The Fab Five—my first unofficial street team, or in other words, my fabulous support group!

The Quad City Scribblers—our meetings revive my writing soul. If only we could travel to the worlds of our imaginations, but at least we have our brainstorming sessions.

My church family and Bible study ladies—I respect each one of you as a wife, mother, and friend. Thanks for all of your prayers as I created this book.

God—I'm so grateful for the opportunity to write *Completely Yours*. Three years ago, if anyone had told me I'd publish short stories about real-life couples, I would've laughed. But you always know better, and I'm forever grateful for all of the couples I've met and for the privilege of sharing their unforgettable stories.

READERS GUIDE

1. Which story captivated you the most? What made it so compelling?

2. What was your favorite romantic moment? *I had to ask. It's a romance, after all!*

3. At some point in every relationship, we must decide whether the relationship is worth it. What makes a relationship worth pursuing? Where would you draw the line?

4. If you could meet any couple in person, which couple would you like to meet?

5. Annie was completely blindsided by Lucas. Have you ever been surprised by a significant other? *Surprises can be good, too!*

6. Why do you think Meghan and Tom decided to renew their vows?

7. Steph had no idea Tony had a crush on her for all those years. What made her finally notice him?

8. Mary had a tough decision to make. Have you ever known anyone who was in a similar situation? What happened?

9. Jenny and Michael met right as their careers were taking off, making it difficult to start a serious relationship. What circumstances make dating difficult? (Age, school, careers, fears, etc.)

10. After Chris' death, it snowed so many times that Sarah believed the snow was a sign from him. Have you ever felt like a loved one was giving you a sign?

11. I witnessed Ryan's proposal to Lyra in person. It melted my heart when he said, "Like the beast in the play, I have found my beauty." Have you ever witnessed a proposal?

12. Which couple could you relate to the most? Explain.

13. Do you believe in true love? Why or why not?

ABOUT THE AUTHOR

Crystal Joy is a stay-at-home mom with a heart for people. She loves getting to know them, writing about them, and inventing them. When she's not hanging out with her hero and heroine in her latest romance, she enjoys discussing politics with her husband, being silly with her little ones, and drinking endless amounts of coffee.

You can learn more about Crystal Joy at her website www.crystaljoybooks.com. If you want to sign up for her newsletter, "From My Heart to Yours," you'll receive exclusive giveaways, opportunities to enter contests, and noteworthy news. Go to this link to sign up: http://eepurl.com/cHgfZ9

You can also connect with her at:
Crystal@Crystaljoybooks.com
facebook.com/profile.php?id=14817699
twitter.com/CrystalJoyBooks
pinterest.com/crystaljoybooks

Coming soon...

Shackled Heart, a romance novel

After losing his wife in a horrific car accident, Charlie Grimm believes that he deserves to pay for the life he stole. Haunted by his irreversible mistakes, Charlie vows he'll never fall in love again, and who could see past his criminal conviction anyway?

MacKenna Christensen strives to support all of her parolees. But when she discovers Charlie is her client, she refuses to help him. She can never erase the gruesome images of his wife's death from her memory. Yet when she sees Charlie's anguish, she realizes he's not the reckless monster she imagined.

As the disdain between Charlie and Mac turns to desire, guilt tears them apart. Is Mac willing to take a chance on a client at the risk of losing her job? Can Charlie forgive himself and open his heart to Mac, or will she become one more regret?

Made in the USA
Middletown, DE
06 January 2020

82611270R10128